DEMISE OF THE DAME

DEMISE OF THE DAME

DENNIS MOSSBURG

Acknowledgments

I start by thanking my awesome wife, Margo. From reading early drafts to giving me advice on the cover to keeping me true to my voice she was as important to this book getting done as I was. Thank you so much, dear.

A special thanks to my mom, Marie Clifner who resurrected Hayden and provided valuable feedback.

Heartfelt thanks Amanda Estep, Sheryl Hammons, Darcy Byrne, Sue Beach, and Pam McDermott for the feedback.

Sincere thanks to our dogs for helping me remember the important things.

Finally, to the readers who embark on this adventure with me. You can help others go on this adventure by leaving a review on your favorite book seller site.

CONTENTS

Acknowledgments   iv
Dedication   viii

1 The Dame   1

2 The Friends   7

3 The Autopsy   12

4 Nora   16

5 The Newshawk   20

6 The Elite   23

7 The Reality Check   27

8 The Note   30

9 The Senator   34

10 The Club   40

11 The Dance   44

12 Thunder and Lightning   47

13 Wakey Wakey   50

14 What If   53

15 The Morning After   56

16 The Playboy   60

17	The Yegg	64
18	The Dungeon	67
19	Internal Affairs	71
20	George Fox	75
21	Chief Hewitt	81
22	Downing University	85
23	June Kayer	89
24	Nancy Mason	94
25	The Roadhouse	99
26	The Arizona	104
27	Calluses	106
28	Vincent Largo	109
29	Spragg	113
30	The Cemetery	117
31	The Funeral	120
32	Puppets	123
33	The Big Fish	128
34	Guido	131
35	Burkholter	134
36	The Fight	137
37	The Tail	140
38	The Stash	146
39	A Thousand Words	149
40	The Brute	152

41 Second Chances   157

42 Trophies   159

43 Cornered   163

44 The Negotiation   169

45 Bent Cops   171

46 The Debt   174

47 Epilogue   177

About the Author   179

Here's to the dame who keeps me on my toes.
She can solve the case of the missing socks, yet can't answer the question, "Where did that dog come from?"

CHAPTER 1

The Dame

The pop of flashbulbs, and the shocked faces told me, I was at either a Hollywood movie premier or a murder scene. The last actor I'd seen was Suzy Kingsman from my high school's drama club. I was voting for the murder scene.

Dying to figure out which it was, I scanned the room, looking for the beautiful celebrity or the body. Turns out it was both.

It was about two in the morning. I got the call half an hour ago. The desk sergeant didn't give any details. He told me to get over to an address in the hills, where doctors, lawyers and other big-time crooks live. I knew the case was going to be political from the address alone. When I saw the victim, I realized how much trouble I was in.

This was Lila Glisan, daughter of Judge Glisan. The good news, he was not a judge anymore. The bad news, he had become a US Senator.

When Roosevelt won a third term, Judge Glisan knew that as a conservative he would never get a Federal bench. He accepted a vacated Senate seat.

Among those who care about such things, there was a debate about his new title. He had been a judge so long that some people were unwilling to drop the "Judge." Others switched and called him Senator Glisan. Those who dealt in sarcasm called him Senator Judge Glisan.

Lila came to Senator Judge Glisan late in life. When she was born, his older children were already in college or the last year of high school. Glisan doted on his little girl. She did not have to make do the way most everyone else did during the war. She even had the luxury of nylons during the war.

As far as I know, she never did anything. She went to college only as much as she had to so daddy would keep paying the bills. And she never had to work.

I had that wrong: she did lots of things, but nothing worth a damn.

Her photograph was often in the society pages of the newspaper. She was always attending some social function, dressed to the nines. The gossip columnists made it their mission to track the men she dated and speculated about if this was "the one."

Women in their twenties wanted the men she had. Teenage girls wanted the clothes she wore. And men wanted those clothes off.

Those men would not want to see her now. Her body lay naked on the living room floor. Her arms and legs spread out forming an X. Her red insides provided a nice accent to the tan rug and her creamy skin. I guess she did have a way with colors.

All around me people went about their jobs. Lab guys collected evidence. Photographers documented the scene. Uniforms were maintaining the perimeter around the house and questioning neighbors. They would say that she was a nice girl and they couldn't imagine why someone would do this to her. You hear it so often you wonder if there's a playbook somewhere. It's in the chapter, *When Heinous Crimes Happen to Good People*.

With all this activity going on around me, I stood in the space between the foyer and the living room. Why was I here? This had to be a mistake. That or I was being set up. I was on-call this week but the desk sergeant should have called the lieutenant or even a captain. This was not a murder scene, it was the site of a media feeding frenzy.

There's a hierarchy for murder victims. A transient might rate a uniformed officer. The average Joe gets a detective. A rich cat gets a detective sergeant and a detective. The higher up the vic goes, the more attention they get. Lila rated a captain, his subordinates and an early morning call from the chief. He would stop by the scene wearing a trench coat over his pajamas to tell us what a good job we're doing. Then he would go home, put down a few shots of whiskey and wonder what he's going to tell Senator Judge Glisan.

I found the officer in charge of the crime scene. It was Sgt. Langella. I knew him. He was a good sergeant.

"Is the lieutenant on his way?"

He laughed. "No. Do you need him to hold your hand?"

"What do we know?"

"She was due at a party. When she didn't show some of her friends called, but she didn't answer. They came over and let themselves in with a key one of them had."

I tried to imagine what they thought when they, half drunk, opened the door and saw her hanging out here. That would sober them up.

"How are they doing?"

"Pretty shook. They're cooling their heels in the kitchen."

"You give them something to calm down?"

He looked at me. His mouth opened, then he closed it. After a moment he said, "I thought they should be sober for you detective. I had the guys take all the alcohol out of the kitchen and put on a pot of coffee.

"Thanks."

"Yeah."

Her friends were waiting for the great detective to make everything better. I didn't know how to do that. If this were a regular case, I would proceed as usual: that being the definition of a regular case.

This was far from the usual. These cases always had a game plan that went one of three ways. The first option was to make it go away so as not to cause harm and embarrassment to Senator Judge Glisan and family.

Second, I could round up the usual suspects. Beat the crap out of them until one of them confessed, whether he was guilty or not. He would go to the concrete mama where he would dance at the end of a rope.

Or third, I could treat this like any other case. I had to hope that someone higher up did not have one of the other options in mind.

I settled on the last option. I was already here and I had my second best suit on, that being the $5 one. I may as well do my job. Besides, if I did choose the wrong option, what could they do? Take away my birthday?

I walked down the two steps separating the foyer from the living room to talk to Dr. Davison. He was from the pathologist's office. Like me, there was someone higher up who should have been here.

"How long?"

He ran his fingers through his thinning hair. Whenever I thought my job was tough, all I had to do was thinking of Davison, 28 and already going bald. And the hair that refused to give up the fight was turning grey.

"Tough to tell, the way she's cut open, body temperature dissipates faster. Rigor is starting to set in, so I would say two to four hours."

She was in the middle of the floor. There was a leather couch on her left, parallel to her torso. A fireplace was opposite, on her right. Chairs matching the couch flanked the fireplace. Coming down the steps, I ended up at her feet.

Someone had removed her internal organs from her torso, but they were still attached to the body. Blood had pooled around her torso soaking into the carpet.

I looked back at Davison. "Anything missing?"

"Don't think so. Dr. Burkholter will perform the full autopsy tomorrow." Burkholter was the county's lead pathologist. Burkholter should have been here instead of Davison.

I walked around the body examining it from all angles. There was little room between her arms and legs and the furniture.

When I reached her left hand, I crouched down for a better look. There was a bruise ringing her wrist.

"She has those on both wrists and ankles," piped up the good doctor.

"Rope?"

"Appears that way. There wasn't any when I got here."

"Langella?" I called out.

"Yeah?" he responded coming into view from the hall to my (and Lila's) left.

"You or anybody find any rope here?"

"No. Say, you wanna talk to her friends?"

"Yeah. Give me a minute."

I looked back at the hand, noting broken and jagged, red nails. The right hand was the same.

"Remember to check under her nails." I told Davison. It was unnecessary, he knew his job. If I didn't say something and it wasn't done, somebody would decide to tack my hide to the wall. I was kind of attached to my hide. I would hate to see anything bad happen to it. So I made sure everybody did their job.

I continued my examination of the body. Stopping at her feet, I asked, "Rape?"

"Don't think so."

I was asleep less than an hour ago. I had only been asleep about ninety minutes. My mind was doing its best to figure this out and failing. Something was wrong here. I mean besides the disemboweling.

I moved to the fireplace surveying the living room. Besides the other furnishings, there were end tables with lamps on them. Pictures in frames, the obligatory doilies, and potted plants.

I asked the photographer how many rolls of film he had shot. He told me. I told him to shoot another. This time of the living room without regard to the body. I told Davison he could move her whenever he was ready.

I moved to the hall to stand next to Langella. I took one look back at Lila as Davison finished his duties.

"Was she covered with a blanket or anything by her friends?"

"No." I must have been too tired for my poker face to be in full force. "I thought it was odd too," he said.

"Have you talked to her friends?"

"No. We have their names and that's it." He gave me the names. I recognized one of them. She was also a regular in the society pages. The others I didn't know from Adam and Eve. I thought it was time I introduced myself.

CHAPTER 2

The Friends

Sally Kaufman was not as attractive nor as well placed as her friend Lila. This meant her photo only made it in the paper as a background feature to Lila, the star. That is not to say that Sally was in danger of winding up a 90 year-old spinster having to eat at a soup kitchen.

Sally's father, Bill was the Speaker of the House in the state legislature for ten years. He seemed poised to run for Governor, so she knew some prestige. Her maternal grandfather, Jackson Alexander, made a fortune in the lumber industry. That may not seem important in this age of steel. In the timber age, McLoughlin, Pittock, and Jackson ran the world.

Having no interest in the lives of the rich and famous, I did not know how Lila and Sally had become friends. I also did not know the true depth of thier friendship.

Sally moved around the kitchen preparing coffee and wiping up nonexistent messes. I didn't know she had a domestic side. She wore a black evening gown. A couple sat at a small table. The man wore a black jacket, thin black tie and a white shirt. The woman wore an evening gown. They all turned to look at me.

"I'm Detective Hayden. I'm here to investigate the death of Lila Glisan."

"I would have thought you here to write me a parking ticket. I'll sleep better knowing you are on the job." This was from the man at the table. On his chin he sported a brush of whiskers. In some circles, I'm sure he looked stylish. To me he looked like a mortician who missed a spot while shaving.

"Was that your Nash parked out front?" I took his flaring nostrils to mean yes. "It was in the way. I had it towed." His eyes got larger. "It will be in the impound yard in the morning. What will we find in there?" I didn't have the car towed. I wanted to jerk his chain some and see what dropped out.

He brought a cigarette he had been smoking up to his mouth, took a long drag, and blew smoke in my direction. I looked at Sgt. Langella who stood behind me and to my left. Our eyes met and after the briefest of moments, he left.

Langella had been a sergeant longer than I had been on the force. He knew the drill

I hated smokers, they reminded me of my old man. I never once saw him without a cigarette in his mouth. He had many other redeeming qualities: his life was solitary, poor, nasty, brutish, and short. Hobbes would have been proud.

"Never mind Carl, detective. He spends his time thinking. When he does come out of his ivory tower, he does not know how to act in polite company," Sally said. "May I offer you a cup of coffee?" I said she could and black was fine. I took the coffee and set it next to my hat, which I had laid on the tile counter.

"You were to meet Lila at some event?" My question met with cautious silence. Sally stood at the sink rinsing cups. Carl crushed out his cigarette in an ashtray next to three other cigarette butts, and lit another. The other chick looked at Carl.

"Nancy? Where were you supposed to meet Lila?" She turned her big doe eyes to me, then looked to her hands in her lap. From Sgt. Langella's list, I knew this had to be Nancy Mason. And that's why they made me a detective.

"A party with some friends." I didn't know Nancy, but I had met girls like her before. She had the nice clothes, but her Sunday best did not quite match up to Sally's or Lila's. Right now, she looked a lot better than Lila.

She was cute, but not a beautiful girl. She hung with those more glamorous ladies who let her. Girls like Nancy never quite figure out that beauty only lasts so long. And arrogance destroys it.

"Look Nancy, I don't care what you did at this party, I'm trying to figure out what was going on. Could someone at this party have noticed that Lila was not there? Could that someone have come over here to take advantage of her? Am I off base?"

"How dare you accuse our friends of doing this, this, heinous act."

"Carl, I didn't accuse anybody. I threw out a suggestion. It's my job. But the way you're all acting, I know you were up to something. Unless it has something to do with Lila's murder, I don't care what it was. But I may care if you keep acting like an asshole. Sorry ladies."

"I'm sorry, I guess I'm on edge. We were at a cotillion. Sort of a spring festival."

"How many people were at this cotillion?" Who in the world speaks like this?

"Two hundred, three hundred. Something like that."

"Who put on the shindig?" Sally and Nancy looked again at Carl. He was trying to regain his cool without annoying me again.

"Cormack McCollum. It was at his mansion."

"Who found Lila?"

"I did." Sally spoke without looking at Carl.

"You're the one with the key?"

"Yes. In case she locked herself out or lost her key."

"And when you saw her?" Still facing me, her eyes wandered to Carl.

"I never thought anyone would do something like this to her."

"She didn't have any enemies?" They all shook their heads. "You can't think of anyone who would do this?" More head shaking.

I waited. Then I waited some more. I could do this all day.

Nancy studied her hands in her lap and rocked back and forth. Carl had created a dense cloud of smoke around himself. Combustion was eminent. Sally wiped down the counter. Despite her best efforts, the glaze wouldn't come up from the tile.

Langella returned and interrupted our stalemate by clearing his throat. When I looked at him, he shook his head. He hadn't found anything.

"Well if anyone thinks of anything, you can reach me at Central. I'll ask you not to leave town for a while in case I have any more questions."

I grabbed my hat from the counter sweeping the cup of coffee off the counter. When it crashed to the floor, Nancy jumped like someone shot her. Carl paused with his cigarette six inches from his mouth. But Sally sprang into action.

She asked if I was OK and shoved me out of the way. She picked up the shards, then walked straight to the pantry. She returned with a mop and began cleaning up the coffee. She seemed to know her way around the kitchen for someone who didn't live here.

When she had everything cleaned up, I escorted them outside. Davison had removed Lila's body. It did not keep all eyes from turning to the living room, looking for her.

The newshawks, neighbors and gawkers had moved along to find something else to glom on to.

Carl's Nash was still outside but not in the condition he had left it. It was not even in a condition he would recognize. It now sat on its brake drums. The tires were next to it. The doors, hood, and trunk were all open. Contents from the trunk were on the street behind the vehicle. The seats were out of the car taking up the street and sidewalk. Parts of the engine resided outside the vehicle. It looked very much like an automotive version of Lila.

The effect on Carl was spectacular.

"You. You," he sputtered up at me before turning back to the car and screaming.

"Look on the bright side, we didn't find any drugs in your car." I didn't think Langella and crew would find anything. Hanson had the smell of bad news. It might have been his cologne.

He was halfway down the walk when he turned back to me.

"You're not going to get away with this. I'll have your badge!" He stormed up to me again shaking a finger in my face. "I know people. You're done."

"I know people too. This is Sally Kaufman. She's Nancy Mason. You're Carl Hanson. And the gorillas in uniform on either side of you are officers Andrews and Willis. They will be your escort home tonight. You can come back in the morning and pick up your car."

In the street and porch light, I saw a vein sticking out on Carl's forehead. The way it was throbbing, I expected it to explode. His jaw muscles bulged. I expected to hear his teeth breaking. "This is not over."

"Oh goody, something to write in my diary."

The officers lead the group away to a police car. They would take everyone home. Note the addresses and give them to me. I didn't know if they were up to something. After their performance in the kitchen, I wasn't so sure.

CHAPTER 3

The Autopsy

I spent another hour in the house, searching and thinking over the crime. Who would want Lila Glisan dead and why? Was it something to do with her father? Could someone he sentenced be seeking revenge? But why not go after Senator Judge Glisan, instead of his daughter?

I also could not help but wonder about Carl Hanson. I didn't have to antagonize him. I'm not sure why I did. That's a lie. I know why. I wanted to see the smug little jerk squirm. I wanted to poke him some, see what he would do next. He knew something. It may not have been about the murder, whatever it was, it might be worth sinking my teeth into.

I found no sign of burglary or struggle. Lila was a clean and tidy little socialite. The cupboards in the kitchen were all organized. The plates, dishes and silverware matched. The floors were all clean. Except the living room floor, where I found a large bloodstain. There were plants everywhere. They were all alive. She wasn't trying hard enough.

The cleanliness extended to her bedroom. There weren't any dirty clothes piled in a corner. The closet was organized and the bed made in both bedrooms. There was a spare bedroom which had a closet as well stocked as the master bedroom. I guess she liked clothes.

What bothered me the most was how clean it was. How does a person killed in her own home manage to make it look like she's been the only one in the house?

My mind was running in circles. I went home to catch a few hours of shuteye.

In the morning I was more or less bright eyed and bushy tailed for the autopsy.

Burkholter was not your usual croaker. He had diced up more stiffs than other croakers had cared for living patients. Because of this he had a nonchalant view of life. He thought nothing of displaying organs to even the casual observer.

He also had the habit of looking at you as if to determine how soon you too would end up on the slab. In spite of the fact that the good doctor was very close to a section eight, he was a nice person. He was completely unaware that he creeped everyone out.

"Hayden, it's good to see you. We're finishing this one. We'll get to yours in a minute." He held out a blood-covered hand.

"Uh, no thanks doc, I'll wait for breakfast." He looked at the hand.

Seeing the blood, he wiped it on his smock several times, then plunged it back into the stiff he was working on.

"I'll be out here," I said and walked back out to the hall.

I had seen him in action enough that Burkholter no longer bothered me. I went out to the hall to see who else might show up. I was still cooling my heels alone when Davison stuck his head out of the office to tell me they were ready to begin.

Autopsies did not bother me. I have seen many since becoming a detective. Seeing the organs removed. Seeing the body sliced open. Getting a close up view of the sometimes, horrible wounds suffered. None of that bothered me.

What does bother me is seeing the body on the steel slab before the whole thing begins. The blue lips and fingertips, the pasty white skin. The dark purple lividity from pooling blood. A few hours before, that body was walking around.

She had purpose. She had hopes and dreams. None of that was any help to her now. She had crossed that threshold separating person and thing.

Burkholter began by examining the body, pointing out signs of external trauma. He spoke into the microphone of one of those new reel-to-reel tape recorders. I guess it's easier than jotting notes for your report with blood on your hands.

Which reminded me; I did not need to be there. I could read the report as well as the next guy. Burkholter knew what was important and what wasn't. I did not need to go to most autopsies. In this case, given the name of the victim, I had to be here. Justice is blind, to all things except class and cabbage.

Burkholter gestured to Lila's sliced open abdomen and said, "They did most of the hard work already." He laughed at his own joke.

"Were you ever in Vaudeville, doc?" Davison had packed Lila's organs back in her abdomen last night to transport her here. Burkholter started unpacking them.

"Anything missing?" I asked as he examined the internal organs.

"No, not that I can see. Whoever did this did a good job."

"Do you mean 'good' as in you are glad they did it or skillful?"

"Skillful. Get close here. Have you ever seen such handiwork? Why the organs weren't even touched when they sliced her open."

"You think this is the work of another croaker?"

"Could be. Remarkable, all the organs are still connected."

"Fascinating," I replied stifling a yawn.

He looked up from the body. "I'm not sure you realize what this means."

"Why don't you put me wise?"

"She was still alive when this happened. She died from strangulation, not from the removal of her organs." I thought about what he said while he continued to dig through Lila's organs.

"I thought someone had tied her up at the wrists and ankles to rape her. Did they tie her up to do this?"

"Yes. There are no signs of rape."

This case was all wrong. Things like this didn't happen. I usually in-
vestigated gangland hits, victims of wife beaters, bodies of wife beaters. I
was treading into uncharted waters, and this shouldn't even be my case.

"She had rice for dinner. Here smell." Burkholter was holding
swollen pieces of undigested rice under my nose.

I inhaled. "Like mom used to throw away." Burkholter laughed.

"That's what I like about you Hayden. You're not queasy like some
of the other cops we get in here."

"That's what I like about you doc, you're not sane like most of the
other croakers I know. Say doc, she have any drugs in her system? This
would be painful to go through and she wasn't gagged."

"I won't have test results back for a while, but I see what you mean."

We both walked to the end of the slab where her head rested. I saw
no creases or other sign someone had gagged her. Burkholter reached
down, opening her mouth.

"Well Hayden, they didn't have to gag her. They had already cut out
her tongue."

CHAPTER 4

Nora

As I said, I'm an old hand at autopsies, but that bit about her tongue ended my interest. I told Burkholter I would read his report. A missing tongue would not be enough to drive me away. That combined with everything else made me want to find some other job.

I considered my prospects. And I thought about my skills. And I realized there weren't a lot of jobs for sarcastic pessimists. So, I thought I would see if eating some breakfast would make things any better.

I went to a hash house. It's not a cop joint, which is fine with me. Other cops are always cops; they eat, drink and sleep cop life. I need a change sometimes.

Coming out as I was going in was Nora Hamilton. The dame was one lollapalooza. Long red hair, creamy skin, green eyes. Getaway-sticks that would make a priest reconsider. And curves that would make a Le-Mans driver nervous. "When are you going to ask me out tall dark and brooding?" We both eat at Frank's regular. We had spoken a few times. I had asked her out once or twice. She always seemed to be with another beau. It didn't stop me from making eyes at her.

"I'm over you Nora. Last night I was in the presence of a beautiful, naked celebrity."

"Dead women don't count Hayden. Don't be so surprised. It's in the paper. I'm not seeing anyone now."

"How about tonight?"

"Tonight might not be good. I have to work late. But why don't you give me call?" She gave me her number. We said our good-byes.

I took my hat off when I entered. I made my way to my usual spot, at short end of the 'L' shaped bar where I could glom over the whole room. I ordered biscuits and gravy and started reading the rag Frank had left for me.

As Nora had said, Lila's death was on the front page complete with crime scene photos. It wasn't Lila's crime scene, but it was a crime scene. It was of a young lady with her face covered.

The story cited an unnamed source "close to the investigation." This source said the police had some solid leads and "arrests should come soon." That was refreshing to hear.

Frank brought the gravy and biscuits and the requisite eggs.

"Say Frank, do you need a cook who can't cook?"

"Sorry, I do all the cooking."

"So you already have one eh?" I asked, dipping some egg into the gravy.

"Sad business huh?" he asked, nodding to the paper.

"Yeah, but 'arrests should come soon. '" I had never told Frank I was a snooper, but he had figured it long ago. I guess only mob boys and cops wear guns in shoulder holsters. I never flashed much cabbage, so I must be a cop.

"Sure, that's why yer eatin' biscuits and gravy. You never eat that when 'arrests should come soon. '" Frank walked back to the grill to prepare someone else's slop du 'jour.

I read the paper as I finished my breakfast. I stopped at the crossword to display to the next person that my vocabulary was not as big as I had thought. I finished my coffee (I didn't suspect Frank of anything, so I refrained from breaking the cup). I paid, leaving as much a tip as my salary allowed. I thanked Frank for allowing me the opportunity to get sick and left.

It was going to be a good day, weather wise at least. I put my lid on, looking up at the sky. It was clear and almost 70 degrees already and it was only 9:30.

On my way to the station, I thought about my talk with the captain. I would be willing to hand this case over to someone more capable politics wise. But if I were right, it would not be necessary. He'd pull me after looking over the preliminary reports. I'm not the person who would play the game right way. Hell, I wouldn't even play the game.

I was telling myself that when I walked into the office.

A few of the guys looked up and said, "Hi."

"Does Cap want to see me?" I asked nobody in particular. When someone told me that the captain had not asked for me, I thought that it must be an oversight. I walked to his office and knocked.

"Come in. Oh, hi Hayden."

"Did you want to see me Cap?"

"No. Why?"

"Did you see the case I got last night?"

"How could I not? It's all over the paper. How are you coming on it?"

"That's what I wanted to talk about. Is there someone else you would rather have on this case?"

He looked puzzled.

"Why? It's a murder. Isn't it?"

"A murder? Are you nuts? This is a political time bomb ready to go off in my face. If Chief Bowers has a game plan, you should put someone on it who will follow the plan."

He laughed. That put me at ease. "That's what this is about? Hayden, you are one of the best I have. Treat it like any other case." He sounded definite, but I thought I'd try again.

"You haven't got any calls from the Senator's or the Mayor's office?"

"Of course I have. I told them I had my best man on it. If you need any help from me or the other guys, ask."

"Thank you." I opened the door and paused. "Is the esteemed Senator Judge Glisan in town?" Cap looked up at me. With his hand still resting on the desk, he gestured for me to come forward. I closed the door and stood in front of his desk.

"Hayden, your flaw is that wise attitude of yours."

"Whatever do you mean?"

"I'm not going to sit here and play with you. Senator Glisan is in the District or he was last night. He is on his way here now and should be in tonight or tomorrow morning.

"He wants to speak with you when he makes it into town. When you meet him, be respectful. Do I need to remind you that he has many connections to the department?"

"Of course I'll be respectful. He's got an iron clad alibi."

"Hayden, if you worked for anybody else you wouldn't have a job."
"That's not true. This morning I turned down an offer at one of the city's finest eating establishments."

"I'm sure Frank would be very happy with an employee who showed up for work at 10 in the morning. Now get out of here and find out who did this."

CHAPTER 5

The Newshawk

After a detour to the water cooler, I went to my desk. On it I found a manila envelope marked, "Crime Scene: Lila Glisan." I moved it aside.

I spent the next few hours working on other cases. Unlike those detectives in the movies, real detectives have to work on more than one case at a time. We also find it easier to use the phone than to drive all over town.

Captain Bartholomew made it clear that I was working the Glisan case. I didn't have a problem with working the case. If Cap wanted me to work it, that was fine with me. I did wonder how Senator Judge Glisan felt about a lowly detective working the case. I didn't give a damn. I did give a damn about who killed his daughter.

After a few hours on the blower, trying to talk to witnesses, I decided it was time for lunch. Then a visit to McCollum.

There's a hash house near the station named O'Bryan's. It's an OK place. It tends to draw the wrong kind of people, police brass and newshawks. They seem to have some sick symbiotic relationship. The brass will say whatever they have to, to get their asses kissed. Newshawks are happy to kiss ass to get a story.

So, it works out in the end.

I hated the place, but if you wanted to know what was going on in the department, this was the place to go.

I found a table and put my back to the wall. Deloris, one of the waitresses came over and took my order. It was a Ruben.

Business was slow. Only a handful of cops, and a few newshawks, but they hardly mattered.

I opened the manila envelope from my desk. Inside I found Lila's crime scene photos.

"Hey Hayden. Say, is that Lila Glisan? Lemme see." I looked up to see Les Carson, a newshawk for one of the town's morning rags. He was also the author of the fascinating article I read this morning about the murder. I shoved the photos back in the envelope.

"Dust off, Les."

"Now Hayden, this is the biggest news to hit this berg since they caught Mayor Denson with them Boy Scouts. Let me eyeball those pics."

"I'm going to make you wish you had used certain parts of your anatomy when you had the chance, now beat it!" I put the envelope on the table and put my left elbow on it. Carson sat down and slipped into his natural state, that of ass kisser.

"Hayden, I gotta tell you, this case could bring a guy up in the force. A well written story could get the attention of the right people."

"Why would I talk to you then? You don't let the facts get in the way of a great story."

"Why should I? The facts are what I say they are. A hundred years from now are you going to be around? No, but the paper archives a hundred copies of every issue. No matter what the facts are, what I write will be the only record of what happened, it's my legacy. If you want history to smile on you, you should let me on the inside of this story."

"Come on Carson, I want to be able to hold down my lunch. Speaking of which, here it comes. Now fade."

"Well Hayden, if you change your mind, give me a call at the office." He stood and tossed a card down on the table, as Deloris brought my Ruben.

My conversation with Carson had not helped my appetite. I know better than to let a worm like him get under my skin, but somehow, that's what he had done.

I don't give two shakes about a promotion. It's too much paper pushing, not enough fresh air.

What did bother me was the feeling that I had gained a parasite. Newshawks have somehow gotten it into their heads that it is important to be the first with the story. Carson was no different. Until I solved this case, he was going to be doing his best to be my shadow. I needed that like I needed another nose.

I pulled out the photos. They showed the scene as I remember except in glorious black and white. I looked around the room and back at the photos. They were still the same, and Lila was still dead.

Murders are usually simple. Killers may have elaborate schemes to get their victim, but the death is usually simple. A bullet to the brain, a knife to the heart, even a good old-fashioned beating. Those are all things a hood can understand and do.

Lila's murder required finesse. Hoods have about as much finesse as a pig on ice skates.

That ruled out your garden variety revenge hit. Hell, it ruled out about any kind of gang hit, which left me with nothing to go on.

Well, not quite nothing. If this was not a gangland murder, then I could remove the usual suspects from my list. Leaving me with the un-usual suspects.

You have no idea how comforting that thought was.

The Elite

Cormack McCollum's house was right out of a Southern planta-tion. The white house was a two story affair. Six huge columns dominated the front. They supported first and second floor porches. Chimneys broke up the roof line on each end and the middle of the house. All McCollum needed to complete the setting was a black butler.

He didn't disappoint me. A black man in a black suit and white gloves answered the door. We stared at each other for long moments. Me, wondering what the hell was going on. He, well, I'm not sure what he was thinking, except, "Here we go again."

"May I help you sir?" he broke the ice.

"Is McCollum in?"

"I'm afraid not sir." I showed my badge and the tone changed. "I hear the back door. Follow me." He led me to a sitting room. I stood and waited.

The house, continuing the Southern theme, was well decorated. Pale blue walls, Federal furniture and velvet curtains set the scene. In the center of the sitting room was a claw foot table. On it sat a vase with lilac cuttings. Their smell pervaded the whole room. It was the rug that tied the room together.

His house sat on the South Hill affording McCollum a view of the city. I was looking out the large bay window at the city. It was that or look at an oil painting of McCollum riding a horse. The lord of the manor made his appearance.

"Hello detective . . . "

"Hayden."

"Detective Hayden." He stuck out his hand. I shook it then took the seat he had offered. "This is quite the house you have."

"Thank you. When I came to this country I spent the first few years in the south. I fell in love with the architecture."

"And now you are here."

"The silver mines in Idaho drew me here. My father's business is tobacco farming. A friend of mine and I heard about the mines. We were seeking adventure. I got here and saw forests bigger than Ireland and farmland as far as the eye could see."

"You don't have much of an accent."

"I've lived here longer than I ever did in Ireland or the South. May I offer you a drink? A lemonade?"

"My Lord, yes. It's hot out today," I said, fanning myself with my hat.

"Samuel." The butler appeared in the doorway. "Two lemonades."

"Yes sir, Mr. McCollum."

When Samuel was out of the room, McCollum asked, "What may I do for you, detective?"

"Did you have a shindig last night?"

"I did host a cotillion. There was nothing illegal about it though." Samuel brought in our drinks. He held out a silver tray with two glasses with pale yellow liquid. I paused then took one of the glasses. Our eyes met and I wrinkled my nose. His composure cracked for a second. A small smile showed at the corner of his mouth. He left once he served McCollum. I took a sip and sat the glass on the table next to the lilacs, allowing the offending odors to fight it out.

"I didn't accuse you of anything." He swirled his glass, the ice tinkling against the sides.

"A natural assumption, no? When a policeman asks you about something, it's natural for you to think of the legality."

"Did you invite Lila Glisan?"

"I did."

"How about Sally Kaufman, Carl Hanson, and Nancy Mason?"

"Sally, yes. The other two may have been guests of hers. What is this?"

"Did you see any of those people last night?"

"I saw Sally. There were some people with her, they may have been Nancy and Carl. I didn't see Lila. I was hoping to see her."

"Have you read the paper? Heard the news on the radio?"

"The business section. I've not heard any news. Why?"

"Someone murdered Lila Glisan last night." McCollum appeared surprised and upset. He collapsed back in the chair, his face pale, mouth open.

He needed something stronger than lemonade. He stood and walked over to a table behind his desk and picked up a decanter with an amber liquid inside. He picked up the decanter and looked at me.

"I've seen too many men crawl in one of those and disappear."

His face didn't reveal anything. He poured a couple of fingers in a tumbler.

"And if you gaze long enough into an abyss, the abyss will gaze back into you." He raised the glass, tipped it back and stared into the bottom of the glass.

Nietzsche. I don't know how to respond when people quote literature to me. Is it an intellectual's version of talking about the weather? Is he saying it to himself? About himself? Was he testing me?

I let it drift. *They muddy the water, to make it seem deep,* also by Neitzsche.

"Did you know Glisan well?"

"I know her father. I've known him since before she was born. Does he know?"

"Yes."

"This'll destroy him."

"Do you know anyone who would want her dead? Or want to get to him by killing her?"

"No. Someone he'd sentenced?"

"We're checking that angle. How late did Sally and her friends stay?"

"I don't keep track of all my guests. There were a lot of them. I guess about midnight."

"Were they the last to leave?"

"No. The cotillion lasted until about one. This is awful." He poured another drink, swirled the glass and took a drink.

"I'm sure Lila would agree. Anyone else who didn't show up or left very early?"

"No. What are you suggesting? That one of my guests would do this? Do you know who you are talking about? This city's finest, that's who."

"It's easy, I open my mouth and the words come out. I don't know who did this, but I have to cover all my bases. So you can't think of anyone who would want to bump off Lila?"

"I'm becoming offended at your callousness."

"Yeah. Could I get a copy of the guest list?"

"I don't have a formal list made out. I can have one sent to you."

"Could you rattle off some of the names?"

"This has left me a little flustered. I'm going have to ask you to leave. I'll forward a list to you." He stood. I remained seated.

"I have more questions."

"No, not right now. If you will give me a card, I'll have a list sent to you." I stood, dug out a card and handed it to him.

"Thank you for your help."

"I trust you can show yourself out." I told him I could, and did.

CHAPTER 7

The Reality Check

I learned a few things from my visit with Cormack McCollum. First, he is a nice old man. Second, he's very naive, unusual for powerful businessman. Third, he could be shrewd, trying to throw me off the scent. So, I didn't learn anything.

This case had to be part of a plan. This was not a random act. It had to be someone on the inside—at least near the edge—of the cultural elite.

I thought I should go back to the scene of the crime. See if daylight, a few hours of shuteye and food made it appear any different.

Who knew that the manors lining the South Hill would be witnesses to a bizarre three-ring circus?

In center ring ladies and gentlemen, the ring master, Carl Hanson (applause). In the south ring, those lovable clowns, the mechanics. In the north ring, those verbal prestidigitators, the newshawks (more applause). Watch as they turn lies into facts before your eyes.

Hanson's Nash now had tires. It sat behind a tow truck as the driver hooked it up. Fat men wearing small, oil stained clothes were picking up miscellaneous parts.

Les Carson and a few other newshawks recorded the scene for posterity. Shooters snapped photos of the work. None of them were very interested in Hanson or the car. They talked amongst themselves and the shooters were taking photos of the house and not the car.

Hanson was busy. One moment he shouted orders to the mechanics. The next he was explaining to the newshawks how this violated his civil rights.

My day was getting better and better all the time.

One look at the action and I knew that the last place I wanted to park was in front of the house. I parked my Dodge Custom in a spot on the street intersecting Lila's. I watched a moment, then walked into the circus.

The newshawks and their shooters surrounded me. Flashbulbs popped and questions shouted.

"Gentlemen, he is the man who did this to my car. Detective Hayden, would you care to explain to the reporters why you had my car dismantled?"

"Sure Hanson. Carson, get your pen ready. I have some friends in vice who have been trying to bust the city's largest dope ring. Carl Hanson over there matches the description of a known peddler. You see, I was doing my duty to protect and serve by having Hanson's car searched for dope. I'm sad to report that we didn't find any drugs. The investigation is ongoing and we are sure to catch Hanson at something."

"Lies! He's lying."

"Detective Hayden, how is the investigation into Lila Glisan's murder going?"

"Have you made any arrests?"

"Does Senator Glisan know? Have you spoken to him?"

"Gentlemen. Gentlemen," I said, trying to calm the crowd. "You know that I can't comment on an ongoing investigation. I will tell you that we have some leads and we are doing everything possible to find Miss Glisan's killer.

"Now, if you will excuse me."

Newshawks gave way and shouted questions as I made my way to Hanson. When we were face to face, I held his gaze until I knew I had his attention. I leaned in and said, "They don't care about you. Leave it alone or I'll arrest you for obstruction of justice."

Hanson jumped back. "You hear that? Did you all hear that? He threatened me! Go ahead detective. Why don't you repeat what you said?"

"Are you using that dope you've been peddling? I'm the investigator on the story of the century. If they start dragging my name through the mud, do you think I'm going to give them any information? As soon as you leave, they are going to start kissing my ass. They used you. They don't care about you. All they care about is Lila."

Hanson made a few inarticulate sounds, then looked around at the newshawks. "He threatened me!" he shouted. The newshawks looked down at their notes. The shooters had nothing to photograph. The workers scratched parts of their anatomy they shouldn't, at least not in public. Even the birds seemed to have stopped chirping. Carl Hanson realized that the newshawks didn't care about him. They cared about him the same way they cared about the dog pile they stepped in. All they wanted to do was get away from it so it didn't soil anything else.

In a way, I almost felt sorry for him. He was playing a game to which he didn't know the rules and he was beat before his opening move.

Hanson hung his head and walked to a waiting car and drove off. I saw Sally Kaufman sitting in the passenger seat as the car pulled away from the curb.

CHAPTER 8

The Note

I moved to the front door. A couple of boys in blue stood by the door to Lila's house.

I showed them my buzzer.

"Afternoon detective. Nice show you put on out there," one said.

"Amazing, isn't it? One little murder and all sorts of riffraff start moving in. It's enough to ruin a good neighborhood." I looked back at the newshawks still trying to ask me questions. They all stayed about ten feet from the porch, as if there was some invisible line of death they dare not cross. And there was.

"Have they been behaving themselves?" I asked. "Yeah, they only been here 'bout fifteen minutes."

"That's when that little guy showed up with the tow truck," contributed the other.

"Anybody else come by?"

"No. Some gawkers. We got plate numbers." I took the numbers, thanked the boys and walked inside.

The scene was as I remember, except no bodies, dead or otherwise. Instead of lingering, I walked to the kitchen, where I found the back door. Badges were also standing out there. I let them know I was inside and would check out when I left. I didn't want some overzealous bull to come charging in here burning powder because they heard a noise.

I found a phone in the living room. There was residual dusting powder around the phone. I would have to go to crime scene guys and see what they lifted.

I dropped a dime to Central and started a trace on the plate numbers the bulls out front gave me. I knew it would take some time, so I told the lady I would call back later. It was time to get to work.

I stood in the foyer looking over the living room. I opened a window. From outside the perfume of lilac danced in—they're very popular here.

I took out the pics I had of the scene. I started with the pic of the whole scene. That led to the shots of her wrists and ankles.

Moving down to the living room, I placed the wrist and ankle shots in their positions on the floor. I sat in one of the chairs. It would have been impossible to sit in the chair and hold her wrist down. There would not have been enough leverage.

The chair sat against the wall. I stood and picked it up. It was hefty. I set it back down and checked the legs of the chair. I didn't see any marks.

I sat back down in the chair rubbing my face thinking about going to work for Frank. The smell of lilacs drifted past my nose.

I looked at the bloodstain, where a coffee table should have been.

Looking around the living room and foyer area, I didn't see one. Someone could have moved it aside to do the deed. Interesting, but not as interesting as the thought I had.

I got back on the blower, calling Dr. Burkholter.

"Hello?"

"Yeah doc, this is Hayden. Was Lila pretty much drained?"

"Yes, she was. That's not unusual considering."

"How much are we talking about here? It's about nine pints right?"

"Yeah, that's about right." I thanked him and hung up.

My dad took me hunting as a kid. The first time we got a deer it was late fall and there was snow on the ground. Surrounded by white snow, it was easy to spot crimson blood droplets. What I remember most was the blood. It was everywhere. And it was almost impossible not to get at least some of it on you. Now that I was thinking right, I noticed the lack of blood here. I saw no splattering. No spray, no footprints, no hand prints, no smudging.

Cursing myself, I lifted up the rug. On the back of the rug, I found only one small spot where the blood had soaked through. There was a corresponding spot on the wood below.

What I had feared to be true before, I knew to be true now. Lila had been killed somewhere else. Where was she killed? To that, I had no answers, but I knew how she got here.

Peeking outside, I saw that the tow truck was gone. I stepped outside and asked the uniforms if they had noticed the tow company name. One did and told me the name.

I thanked them, gathered my things—including the rug. I had to go see a man about a car.

There was one problem, a certain crowd of reporters. At least one of them had to see the direction I walked up from. He may be staking the area out, waiting for me.

I called in one of the uniforms each from the front and the back, explained the situation. They nodded at my instructions and left. I gave them five minutes then slipped out the back way to my car.

I was right, one of the newshawks noticed me step out of the alley. He let out a cry and ran to his car. I sprinted for my car to find that someone had already been there. Someone had smashed my driver's side window. In the seat was a rock with a note tied to it. I didn't have time to look at it, it would have to wait. I tossed the rock in the passenger seat and the rug in the back. By the time I pulled my car out into the street, two cars were pulling on to the street.

I let the hammer fall on the accelerator and buzzed through the intersection. The timing was perfect. As I cleared the intersection a marked car moved in to block the street. One of my shadows dynamited his brakes to keep from hitting the cruiser. Did I mention that I love the sound of squealing tires? At the same time the other marked car blocked off the street to the west of the house.

By the time everyone turned around and sorted themselves out, I was long gone.

After I put a few miles between me and the circus, I pulled the Custom to the curb and read the note. It was to the point: Let it go.

CHAPTER 9

The Senator

The rock and note bugged me. It shouldn't have; the car belonged to the department. I was getting under Hanson's skin. I planned to burrow in even deeper.

The shop Hanson took his car to was a real dive. The run down building housed two bays and an office. Behind the building was a fenced yard. The fence protected vehicles whose condition ranged from relic to wreck.

The office gave the impression of age well beyond chronological years. The walls may have been white at one time. They were now the yellow brown that can only come from dirt and tobacco smoke. I smelled old oil and grease, bringing to mind an Army motor pool.

All those words could have described the man in the office. He was less than ten years older than me, but looked at least twenty years older.

I told him I wanted to look over Hanson's car. Talking around the cigar, he told me to perform an unnatural act on myself. I grabbed my badge and, held it front of his face.

"How about you let me look at his car and I won't pay attention to any bent cars I see?" The cigar drooped. He became as cooperative as a pavement princess when the fleet's in.

I took one look at the car. I saw enough. I used the blower to call another tow company to have the car towed to the police impound yard. With parts crammed in the car, it was tough to spot any blood or any other sign of wrongdoing. It was enough to impound the car.

While waiting for the tow, I dug around some. I found a newspaper clipping from a scandal sheet in the glove box. A photo of Lila accompanied the story. The photo was of her as she left The Cleo Club (one of the city's classiest gin mills) arm in arm with the beau of the week. It was something I had seen before and almost passed up. I noticed Hanson in the background. With him (though not arm in arm) was Nancy Mason. Behind him was another man, taller — my height.

His eyes were looking toward the camera while his head faced away. He did not want his photo taken — as though he was with them, but did not want anyone to know he was.

Or I was so desperate, I was grabbing at straws.

I followed the tow down to the impound yard and checked the car in. I then called the crime scene people to tell them about the car. I wanted to let them go over the car, but first, I looked in the truck for signs of blood. I didn't see any.

From the yard I went to Burkholter's office. He was gone for the day. I didn't realize how late it was.

I called the office. Cap answered. He informed me that Senator Judge Glisan was in town and wanted me to stop by his digs.

A white butler opened this door. I flashed my tin and introduced myself. He said Glisan was waiting for me and started leading me through the house.

While McCollum's house screamed money, Senator Judge Glisan's whispered elegance. In the foyer a grand mahogany staircase wound down from the second floor. I imagined Lila gliding down those stairs, wowing waiting suitors.

Dark wood was everywhere. I walked past mahogany paneling, floors, and furnishings. Simple lighting and light colored upholstery, balanced the oppressive feel mahogany can give.

From somewhere in the house floated classical music. The closer we got to Senator Judge Glisan's office, the louder the music became.

Arriving at the office, the butler opened the door. He was about to say something. I put my hand on his shoulder. He looked at me. I was looking at Glisan. The old man was listening to Mahler Symphony 1. Movement 3, the double bass solo started. Mahler described this movement as a funeral procession for the hero.

Glisan was standing over the record player. When the bassoon started playing, I took my hand back and nodded my head. The butler announced me and left.

Glisan looked at me, then turned back to the record player. He moved the arm back to its resting place and shut off the player. He turned and motioned to a chair on the other side of his desk.

In the office the lighting was lower and the upholstery was darker. Here, the mahogany threatened, and law books lined the walls. I imagined this is where he met Lila's dates for the first time. This room would leave most people feeling oppressed and in dire straits. I'm not most people.

I moved to the chair and he moved behind the desk. He was about five inches shorter than me, and just as broad. As my father would have said, he's built like a brick shithouse. Not that it bothered me. Kick out the cornerstone and a shithouse will collapse, brick or otherwise. You might end up with some broken toes, but it will fall.

"Nice to meet you Detective Hayden." His grip was firm, eyes strong. Except that he did not wear glasses, he reminded me of Theodore Roosevelt. He had that same presence that said despite his age, he could take most men in a fight.

"Do I call you Senator or Judge?" A small smile crept across his face. If these had been different circumstances, he may have laughed.

"James is fine. And what do I, call you?"

"Hayden." The smile was back, if a little bemused.

I picked up the photo on his desk. It was of Lila standing in front of the house. She was standing there in her dress and pigtails. It looked like one of those first day of school photos.

"Good looking kid even then."

"Thank you. Please sit." He gestured to an overstuffed leather chair beside the desk. "Did you ever appear in my court Hayden?"

"No, James, I was still wet behind the ears when you became a Senator." He nodded and we sat in silence. He had summoned me. I had questions, but right now it was his show.

"Do you have any children Hayden?" I shook my head. "Are you married?" I held up my left hand showing my naked ring finger.

"We had Lila late in life. With our other children, I was not home much; I was working to put food on the table. I was starting my law practice and working long hours. With Lila, I was able to spend more time with her. We became very close over the years. She was the spitting image of her mother, who I buried two years ago.

"Hayden, your captain informs me that you are his best man. I must admit that I hoped the department would throw it's full force at Lila's murder. I trust you will give it your full attention."

We sat in comfortable silence for a few moments before I said, "James, I give every case my full attention. This one won't be any different. I can appreciate the loss of your daughter, but is Joe Blow's daughter any less important than yours?"

Glisan appraised me with his stone eyes. I could not read his face; I didn't know if I pissed him off or if he was reevaluating me.

"You're not afraid of me, are you?"

"No James, I'm not."

"You're aware that I still have many connections in the department?"

"I am."

"What about promotions?"

"If I get one, I want it to be because of my performance, not how well I shove my nose up someone's ass."

He surprised me with a laugh. This was a man who did everything as well as he could. That included laughter.

"I like you Hayden. I threaten you and you still do not back down. I appreciate that in a man. If you are not afraid of me, you're not likely to be afraid of most people. I know you will find my daughter's killer."

"In the interests of full disclosure, I must admit that I am scared to death of my mom." Again, that laugh that seemed to start down low in his gut came boiling forth.

"That's as it should be son. That's as it should be."

I figured it was my turn. "Why did Lila live on her own? There's enough room here."

"It was her idea. Some of the gossip columnists maligned her because she lived at home. She wanted some independence." His head sagged. "If she had still been living here, this would not have happened. There was always someone here. "

"How long has she lived on her own?"

"Eighteen months I suppose."

"Is there anyone who would want to get to you through her?"

"I have thought about that and there are none that I can think of. I did not win many friends as a judge. The same is true now. But I cannot think of anyone in particular."

"Do you know any of Lila's friends?"

"Not as well as I would have liked. Most that I had known, were like her, from wealthy families. I cannot think that any of them would do this."

"Somebody had to do it. Did you see her?" He answered in the affirmative. "I'm sure you know it wasn't your typical goon hit. Something caught up with her. That something was hers or yours."

"What you say may be true. I have told you all I know. I cannot think of anything I have done or am currently involved with that would elicit this response." I drew out the newspaper clipping, and slid it across his desk.

"Besides the obvious, do you recognize anyone in the photo?" He held up the clipping.

"This is Jefferson Parker in the front. The girl is Sally Kaufman. I recognize the man with Sally, but I do not remember his name." He started to hand the clipping back.

"What about the man in the back?" He held it up again.

"I have never seen him before." Glisan handed it back.

"May I talk with your staff who may know her comings and goings better than you?"

"Yes, you are free to do so. Her funeral will be in two days. Would you like to attend?" To my nod, he said: "Very well, I will forward an invitation to your office." We stood and he walked me to the door. "Thank you for coming."

"Hayden. I hope you will keep me appraised."

"Sure, keep reading the paper."

CHAPTER 10

The Club

The long shadow I cast as I walked to my car informed me how late it was, as did the grumbling of my stomach. Lights were popping on in the city below.

It was that time between night and day, when the sun is unwilling to let go of the earth and the night is moving in. Crickets sang a few notes before deciding that night was not here yet. Stars winked, testing the sun. My stomach roared, demanding satisfaction.

In the Custom driving back down the South Hill to town, I thought about my new friend James. When would the other shoe drop? I don't like unwarranted praise. I always wonder what the praiser wants from the praisee. No one acts without his own interests in mind. What did James want?

Did he want anything except the capture of his daughter's killer? He seemed like the kind of guy who played it straight, but I still didn't quite trust him. How could he know so little if he loved his daughter so much?

His staff knew less about Lila's business than he did. I suppose that would stand to reason if she spent little time at her father's house. I still didn't like it.

To get from the South Hill to my apartment, I had to drive through Downtown and that meant The Cleo Club. It wouldn't hurt to check out the joint. There might be food there so I could get my stomach off my back.

A gorilla in a penguin suit stopped me at the door. His face looked like it had been beat into submission by an ugly stick. Scars and calluses decorated his meat hooks.

"Where do you think you're goin'?" the goon asked.

"Thought I'd go in for some grub."

"Not dressed like that you're not." I didn't look down. That might prompt the gorilla to paste me behind the ear. Besides, I knew the condition of my suit. The wrinkled coat matched the wrinkled pants. I was sure that the shirt had seen an iron before I bought it. My tie only had one coffee stain on it, and you couldn't see it in the right lighting: darkness. "Sorry, I left my glad rags at home. I'm sure you understand."

"No, you're not going in." He put a hand on my chest. I grabbed the hand with my thumb in the webbing of his hand. My fingers wrapped around the blade of his hand. I turned his palm to the ceiling. His arm straightened and twisted. I bent his wrist so the palm was facing away from me. He bent at the waist trying to relieve the pressure. I took a step back and he collapsed to the ground on his face and chest. I still held his hand.

"What is it about you meat heads, thinking you can lay hands on people? That's not nice. Now I'm going inside. You're going to leave me alone. Do you know why?"

"Why?" he groaned.

I flashed the tin in his face. I let go of his hand and he stood up rubbing his arm. "Could have said something."

"You should have known. Who else dresses like this?"

It was your typical club. A polished oak bar with an impressive collection of booze bottles along one wall. A bandstand opposite the door and tables around a dance floor. There were booths along one wall. Black and white tiles in a hounds tooth pattern covered the floor. The lighting was low. This was a place for rich cats to catch society chicks.

It was still early for most of the club crowd. The band had set up their instruments, but they weren't playing yet. They must have been waiting in the back.

A young man in a dinner jacket who seemed intent on removing every spot on the glasses tended the bar.

"May I get you something to drink sir?" He asked when I approached. "A wine or a cocktail?"

"Do you have a bar menu?"

"We have appetizers, sandwiches and steaks." He handed me a menu.

I gazed over the menu and ordered a steak. I told him I'd be at one of the booths.

In one corner was a phone kiosk. I figured I'd drop a dime to Nora. By now she may have had dinner already. Maybe she'd come by for drinks. She picked up on the third ring. I propositioned her. She'd had dinner, but drinks sounded fine. She would meet me at the club soon.

I sat at the booth watching as customers filtered in. Single guys stood at the bar. Couples found tables or booths. A couple of waitresses took orders and brought out drinks. A cigarette girl worked the crowd.

"New York, rare?"

"That's me. Thanks."

"You don't want a potato? Or any steak sauce?"

"The potato is filler and sauce distracts from the steaky goodness." She smiled, but she didn't believe me.

I had finished my steak by the time the band came out and started playing some swing music. By now the club was getting crowded and so was the dance floor. The band was good. They were the only colored people in the whole place, except for two men sitting to one side of the bandstand, smoking. Now that I had some food in me and I wasn't so grumpy, I thought I'd go make some friends.

"Samuel, McCollum give you the night off from serving lemonade?" I asked when I reached his table.

He smiled. "The old man likes it. I can't stand the stuff."

I pulled the clipping out of my pocket. "You ever see the guy in the back before?"

"Yeah, I've seen him a couple of times. I don't know his name. Never been to Mr. McCollum's before, but I've seen him here."

"Did Lila and her friends come here often?"

"Couple times a week."

"Was Carl always with them?"

"Nah. He's come on the scene late. Last two months or so. Used to be Lila, Sally and Nancy and whoever their dates were. Then Carl started showing up and that guy in the picture."

As Samuel was talking, Nora walked in the club. Several heads turned, including Samuel's and his friend's.

"Did I say the music was the only reason I came here? Allow me to revise that statement." said Samuel.

I walked across the room and took her hand. We went to my table. I looked at Samuel and he smiled and laughed.

CHAPTER 11

The Dance

A waitress came over to take our drink orders. She took a gin and tonic. I ordered a beer.

"If you are a detective, then why don't you wear a trench coat?"

"Well, you see, I'm a police officer. The trench coat is more of a shamus thing. We flatties usually go with the rumpled suit look." She laughed.

"Have you always been a cop?"

"Yeah. My mom isn't too happy about it. It hurt like hell when she gave birth to me, what with the badge and all."

"Are you like this all the time or is this a special occasion?"

"I could tone it down, but then I'd be as boring as the rest of the palookas in here."

The waitress brought our drinks. I spun my bottle but didn't drink. She looked at hers.

"I shouldn't have ordered a drink. I have to work early."

"I wanted an excuse to be taking a booth." She smiled.

"You were talking about being a cop."

"Actually, I wasn't always a cop. I joined the Army during the war. When the war was over, I came home and got my job back."

"Are you some kind of protector?"

"How do you mean?"

"Well, it's like this: you were here protecting people making peace if you will. Then war breaks out and you help make peace in the world."

"You are trying to make me into more than I am. Japan bombed Pearl Harbor so I went down to the enlistment office the next day."

"Then why are you a cop?"

"Because it pays the bills."

She looked at me a while. Her eyes studying me. Probing me in places I didn't want to go.

"How about you? Did you grow up in Spokane?"

"I'm from Indiana. My family came here when the government started the Hanford Engineer Works."

"Is your dad a scientist?"

"No. He was looking for work. He started as a laborer. Soon he was running equipment, bulldozers and such. My mom was a teacher. I finished high school, then I went to Cheney to attend Eastern Washington College of Education and became a teacher also."

"Where were you when I was in school?"

"I was in another school, getting picked on by another goon."

I asked her to dance. I'm no Fred Astaire, but I managed to keep from mashing her feet too much. She moved with grace that somehow made me forget how clumsy I was.

She smelled like vanilla. Her jade eyes and ruby hair were enough to make a man forget about other dames.

"I have an early day," she said.

"I do too." We danced a little longer.

"I should get home."

"Did you drive?"

"I took a taxi."

"I can take you home."

"Let's go to your place."

With her arms around me, she felt my 1911 in the shoulder holster.

She asked, "Is that a gun in your pocket or are you glad to see me?" I told her it was both.

After we made love, we lay in bed, my arms wrapped around her.

"I've been wondering, why did you go to the War? You were a cop, you were exempt from fighting."

I rolled over, peering into those earnest green eyes. I said: "Because my brother was on the Arizona."

I don't know about bringing peace to the world, but I finally brought peace to the bedroom.

CHAPTER 12

Thunder and Lightning

A long, hard day at work, a full stomach, and a long, hard night. That should have been the recipe for a good night's sleep, but living in a foxhole had left me a light sleeper.

When I heard the footsteps on the fire escape, I rolled off the bed, taking Nora with me. As we rolled off the bed, a Tommy gun thundered outside the room. The next several seconds a cacophony filled the room. The sounds of breaking glass, gun fire and bullets hitting the bed and the wall assaulted our ears.

Nora screamed and tried to get up, tried to get away. I held her down and tried to calm her. I slid one hand between the mattresses. I found the 12 gauge Mossberg loaded with 00 buck.

Cotton batting and plaster rained down on us and Chicago lightning burst over us. When the lightning stopped, I came up over the bed using it for support.

In the window, back lit, was a hatchet man reloading the Tommy gun. He had climbed up the fire escape. Because I was lower than him, I aimed low and fired. The first shot took out his knees. He screamed and fell forward. The next shot took him in the chest. He fell back, his head hitting the rails made a series of sickening thuds as his body fell flat. It didn't matter; he was already dead.

I held my position. Nora had stopped screaming in favor of crying.

Another gunman popped around the window and fired his roscoe. He was screaming. I had seen this in the war. It was usually the last act of a panicked man.

The gink was aiming high. I wasn't.

The shot took him in the gut and the chest. He tumbled over the rail of the fire escape to the street below.

Damn amateurs.

On the street outside I heard squealing tires. I moved to the window, but the boiler was gone. The second gunman had fallen two stories, and made a mess of himself. Lights were coming on in the apartment building across the street. I heard activity in my own building.

Nora sat up. She had stopped crying.

"You must have a jealous boyfriend." She smiled, then the water works started again. I hate it when women cry. I feel that I have failed them in some way. I should have tried harder or done something different. If I had done something different, we would both be dead.

I set the artillery down and picked up a blanket. I sat next to her on the floor and wrapped the blanket around her.

"Everything's Jake. They can't hurt you now." She clung to me like a drowning man to a liferaft.

She asked the eternal questions: "Why? Why did this happen? Why did they do this?" If I knew those answers, I wouldn't have a job. I left the existential aspects to Kierkegaard. The real question became: "Who have I annoyed enough to want to rub me out?"

Today there was Hanson, the wrecking yard owner and the doorman at the gin mill. The last two were in the wrong place at the wrong time. I suspected them of nothing more than general stupidity. Hanson suffered from that, but he was also a suspect in a murder.

Hanson lacked the stones to do something like this. It had to be someone above him. Who was above Hanson? The guy in the clipping? My pal James? Nora? The last two couldn't know me well enough to hate me that much, yet.

Speaking of Nora, her question was even simpler than that. Why did she go on a date with a guy like me?

"Nora, I'm sorry that I put you in this position. This is not an everyday occurrence. Imagine how pissed my landlord would be if it were. Could you imagine the security deposit he would demand?" She gave a subdued laugh as though she felt she shouldn't find humor at a time like this. She slugged me on the shoulder for good measure. She stopped crying. Now it was time for the talk.

"Hayden, you killed those people. I have never been around that before."

"You live by the sword, you die by the sword. Those guys knew the risks."

"You live by it too."

What could I say. "Stay here. I need to look at some things."

The thug on the fire escape had no identification. I would have to make sure the photographer got a good picture of his face.

I slipped on my pants and t-shirt then went down to the street. People in various states of undress backed away from the body.

Careful not to step in splatter matter, I made my way through the crowd. This thug also lacked identification. He also lacked a face. Getting a photo of him would be tough. When he fell, he had twisted so that he came down right on the kisser. Many of my neighbors turned their stomachs inside out when I turned him over.

Damn amateurs.

CHAPTER 13

Wakey Wakey

You can do one of two things when someone tries to put a hit on you. You can castrate yourself and hide in the corner hoping the problem goes away. Or you can find the bastards who ordered the hit and castrate them.

The good news was I had a contract out on me. I had to be doing something right. The bad news was I didn't know who it was.

Hanson didn't have the moxie to order a hit. But he could lead me to whoever did order it.

With uniforms on scene, I went back to my apartment. Nora was waiting in the living room. I came in, and she rushed into my arms.

"Where were you? I was so worried."

"Everything's Jake. Get dressed. You're going home." She liked the sound of that, except she wasn't going anywhere near the bedroom. I brought her clothes out.

While she preened herself, I reloaded the scattergun. She looked at it with questions in her eyes, but didn't ask. When she was ready I escorted her to the street.

On the street, Sgt. Langella was barking orders and taking charge of the scene.

"Creating more work for me, eh Hayden?"

"I gotta do my part to keep you from getting cut down. I need someone to take the lady home and protect her. And I need two of your best to ride shotgun with me."

"You're not leaving me," piped Nora.

"I'll be at your place in an hour. I have to put the screws on somebody to find out who put the curse on me." Nora wasn't happy, but she knew she had no choice.

Langella rounded up Andrews and Willis. Both big guys and Hanson's escort home the previous night. They would go with me, a third officer would take Nora home.

Hanson lived on the third floor of a four-story walk up. His building did not appear to be in as good a shape as mine. Sad considering mine was recently renovated by those fine craftsmen, Thompson and Mossberg. I'm surprised we didn't wake up the whole building as noisy as the stairs were.

We found the door. I listened with my ear to it for half a minute. I heard no activity. What did I expect at two in the morning?

A little magic with my picks and we were in. Andrews and Willis looked at each other, but didn't say anything.

His apartment, was in better condition than the rest of the building. Light from a window in the main room was enough to guide us as we searched for him.

We found him asleep in the bedroom. He was alone. I crossed the room to Hanson's bed. He looked so peaceful like he was having a pleasant dream.

I reached out a patted his cheek. "Hanson. Wakey wakey."

"Wha. What?"

"Who ordered the hit?"

"What?" he asked, blinking sleep out of his eyes. He saw me and sat up in bed, pushing himself back against the headboard. "Detective." He looked at Andrews and Willis and looked back at me.

"Who ordered the hit on me?" I held the shotgun at my side. I wasn't threatening him with it, but his eyes drifted to it.

I reached down and grabbed his goatee. "I don't know what—ouch!"

I had been waiting for an opportunity to do that.

"Now what were you saying?"

"What?"

"Do you remember me? I'm the asshole you've been playing games with. Like smashing out the window of my car."

"I didn't do anything. I've learned my lesson. I'm leaving you alone. I haven't done anything. Ouch." I lifted him up more by this goatee.

"Then who tried to have me aced?"

"I don't know! What are you talking about? Don't hurt me." His words came out like machine gun fire. He was trying to cover long enough to think.

"Some hatchetmen dropped by my place tonight and tried to turn me into Swiss. One of the guys pointed to you. This was before I decorated my wall with his brains. Now what's going on?" He didn't have to know that the buttons couldn't talk.

"I told you! I don't know! I don't know what to tell you." His voice had become a whine. "I didn't ask anyone to kill you. I don't know anything about your car. I haven't done anything to you. Please leave me alone. I don't want to die."

A peculiar odor came to my nose. The front of his pjs were wet.

Looking in his eyes, I saw fear. To my ego's horror, it was not fear of me. He looked to me like he was more afraid of what would happen if he did talk, rather than what would happen if he didn't. I could give him some protection from the world, and a cozy place to think about life.

"You don't want to talk? Fine, let's see if a night under glass, will loosen your lips."

CHAPTER 14

What If

As in most counties, the sheriff runs the jail, but the department runs a lock-up where we can store hoods before interrogation.

I felt sorry for him, so I let Hanson clean up and change. I made him ride with Andrews and Willis.

I told them to get Hanson talking. To play good cop to my bad cop. At the lock-up they told me that they couldn't get a word out of him.

I told the sergeant in charge not to let Hanson have an easy night, but to keep him from getting punked or beat up too much. And to listen in on all his phone calls.

With Hanson tucked away, I went back to my apartment. Everyone was clearing out. I asked the photographer if he snapped shots of the thugs' faces.

He had, and said he would get copies on my desk in the morning.

Langella wanted to know about reports. I told him I would take care of them in the morning.

I found Mr. Ferguson my building super. He had rounded up some wood to cover my window. We had the boards nailed up in a few minutes.

After that I drove to Nora's. I was fifteen minutes later than the promised one hour. She lived in a house built in the '20s in an area that at one time was on the outskirts of town. She told me that she lived with her grandmother, who was visiting friends in Seattle.

The bluebird sat outside in his prowler.

"Anybody been by?"

"Nah. This is a quiet neighborhood. There was this old woman across the street," he gestured with a thumb. "She pulled up a chair and watched from her window waiting for the show. She gave up after twenty minutes."

"There's always one."

"At least."

"Yeah. Thanks for the moll duty."

"Sure thing. Did you get him?"

"Yeah, but I couldn't make him sing. I put him in lock-up for the night. We'll see in the morning." After a few more pleasantries, he took off.

I knocked on the door. There was a long wait, during which, I heard movement inside. The curtain peeled back from the darkened front window.

There was a flurry of movement. The door opened. A woman slammed into me. She wrapped her arms around me and squeezed with incredible strength. It could have been Nora. I wasn't sure. It had happened so fast that I hadn't seen a face. This person was much stronger than I remember Nora being.

"I was so worried." It had to be Nora. The only other woman who worried about me was my mother.

I maneuvered us into the house, closing the door. After a few moments, I managed to disengage from her.

She had cleaned herself up. The smeared makeup was gone. Her eyes were still puffy and surrounded by the natural rouge that accompanied tears. Her evening gown was also gone in favor of a robe with a simple floral pattern. It wasn't one of those old lady robes nor some Mae West special. It was something a librarian would wear.

"So, what happened? Why did you have to go?"

"Well, I got rid of an annoying wart. I found the Lindberg baby and I managed to create world peace." Her face became very stern and she crossed her arms against her chest.

"That's nice, because while you were gone, I vacillated between hugging and slugging you. I'm not sure I made the right choice."

"Fine, I'll go put the Lindberg baby back. Which reminds me: is grave robbing still a crime?" She gave me that scowl that contained a smile.

"I can't believe you said that." She closed the distance between us and slugged me on the shoulder. I wrapped her up in my arms as a matter of self protection.

"Doesn't it bother you that someone tried to kill you?"

"Back to this again." She drew away.

"Yes. I can't believe you're so cavalier about this. We could have died."

"But we didn't. We survived another day. Now, we can stand here and pout about it letting that one moment dictate the rest of our lives or we can move on. I have a dangerous job. I take precautions, but sometimes things happen. I'm sorry that you were there. I'm sorry that your life was in danger, but this is my job."

"It's the thrill isn't it?"

"It was a mistake for me to come here. I'll go back to my bullet-riddled apartment. Tomorrow, we'll see each other at Frank's and we'll wonder, 'What if?'"

"I don't want that."

"Then what do you want?"

"I don't know. Yes I do. I want you. I guess if that means that I'll have to get used to the idea that you are in danger most days, then I guess I will. But you are going to have to promise me something."

"What?"

"Protect your face, I don't want a closed casket funeral."

We kissed. And moved to the bedroom.

CHAPTER 15

The Morning After

Morning came early. It was the sort of morning people get up early for. Light dew coated the grass. High clouds floated overhead inviting dreams of flight. Warm spring sunshine crept across the earth. The sunshine dried up the dew, burned off the clouds, and woke the flowers and the birds. A robin sat on a branch outside Nora's bedroom window lilting, "Good morning," to the world.

I tried to shoot it. Nora stopped me.

Mornings and I aren't on speaking terms anyway. After last night, I was in no mood for those poor jingle-brained who welcome its coming.

"Oh, poor tough guy can't handle a little morning cheer?" she said as she closed the window.

"As a matter of fact, I can't. And do that again and I'll plug you," I said.

"You already have, twice." If it had been later in the day, and my mind hitting on all eight, I would have fired back a witty retort. As it was, all I could manage was a lingering kiss. I tried for more, but she had to get ready for work. A room full of screamers were waiting.

She had already been up and showered. It was my turn. While I was in the rain locker, she fixed breakfast. When I staggered into the kitchen, she was setting the grub on the table: a stack of wheats, eggs, bacon and Joe.

"When do you get off today?" I asked, after downing a piece of bacon.

"About four o'clock," she said, nodding her head.

"You want to have dinner? I don't know any classy joints, but I'm sure I could find a steak place between now and then."

"You are a charmer." I shrugged, still chewing on pancakes and eggs. I gestured at her with a piece of bacon.

"Those palookas at the club last night, I'm sure had charm, but would they have gotten you shot at on your first date?"

"You think women dream for that to happen?"

"Hey, I thought dames loved it when men fought over them." I downed some java washing down the pancakes.

"We also love it when we're called dames. Why don't you call about noon, that's when the children take lunch. I'll be at Keystone 5309."

"Noon huh? You're putting the screws on me time wise, aren't you?"

"You're a detective, that should be enough time for a big tough guy like you. "

We finished eating. I helped her with the dishes. Then she had to go. I asked if I could stay and make a few phone calls. That was fine with her, I had to lock up when I left.

On the doorstep, I kissed her goodbye.

The house was nice, but it was her grandmother's. The furniture was old, a lot of wood and little metal. Doilies and lace were everywhere. An upright piano waited in the front room for someone with a keen ear and adroit fingers to bring it to life. My fingers did their best work when curled into a fist. I wasn't the right man for that job.

I found the phone on a little table next to a davenport in the front room. On a shelf near the floor sat a phone directory. I looked for Jefferson Parker, Lila's arm decoration in the clipping. I was not surprised that I didn't find his name.

I called the desk sergeant at Central. After identifying myself, I asked him to lookup Parker in the city directory. He provided me with an address for a penthouse downtown.

He lived in the Parker building. Don't be so surprised, his dad built it. Except for the penthouse, the building was a posh office building.

There was so much marble, it would have made Caesar's mouth water. I went through one of the sets of revolving doors.

The foyer was cavernous. Potted palms were on each side of the entry providing enough shade to grow mushrooms. The floor was grey marble with a big square of black marble. One corner pointed between the sets of revolving doors. The opposite corner pointed to the security desk in the distance.

White marble columns stretched up to touch the ceiling. Light radiated down from somewhere above.

I took a step. A clomping sound echoed off the walls. I looked around to see who had dropped the safe. To my surprise I discovered I made the sound while wearing soft soled shoes.

I clomped my way across the great divide to the desk. Behind the desk was a hallway with elevators lining each side. The guard sat there in his pretend police uniform, a taskmaster face displayed. I showed him my real badge.

"How's it going this morning?"

"Fine. What can I do for you this morning detective?" he asked as the taskmaster left his face.

"You know Jefferson Parker?"

"Not well. What's he done? This has something to do with the Glisan dame, huh?" We're talking about the son of the guy who signs this guard's paycheck, and he was willing to sacrifice him to a cop. What wonderful dogs they are, always willing to please.

"Did she come over often?"

"I work the dayshift. I only saw her a time or two as she left in the morning."

"So you never talked to her?"

"Nothing more than hello and goodbye."

"Does Parker bring women home often?"

"Sure, he's a real playboy."

"Is he in now?"

"I haven't seen him leave. Let me give him a ring."

"Thanks." It's eight in the morning. Jefferson is probably sleeping off a hangover.

The phone must have rung fifteen times before Jefferson answered. The guard spoke a few sentences then listened to a few. He hung up.

"He'll see you. Take elevator six." He gestured to the bank of elevators on his left.

CHAPTER 16

The Playboy

The ride up in the elevator was fun. It reminded me of many other rides in many other elevators, except this one was posh. This one had brass and marble. How could I forget the ivory buttons? Not that I had to press any buttons. When I stepped on the elevator, the doors closed and we went up to the penthouse.

The doors opened. I stepped out into Xanadu for playboys. The pad had a view of the city from a bank of two story windows that took up one wall. One of the windows was actually a sliding glass door, leading out to a balcony. A rock fireplace ruled the wall across from the elevator. A couch with soft pillows sat in the center of the sunken living room. Opposite the windows was an open kitchen, dining area and stocked bar. Stairs curled around to a loft and more rooms.

There was no butler to greet me. Instead, Jefferson Parker himself greeted me. Pity, I was getting used to butlers.

Parker was the type who reminded you of a movie star. Chiseled chin, complete with a dimple. His blond hair combed despite the early hour. Blue eyes shining despite the late night. I hated him.

"Detective Hayden. Nice to meet you." He stuck out his hand. I shook it. It wasn't firm and it wasn't limp, it was there. "Hat rack is right there." He gestured with a finger. "Have a seat." He waved a hand past the living room. "Coffee?" he asked, gliding in his silk robe to the kitchen. I would have hated to break a cup and stain something.

"No thanks." I followed him to the kitchen. As he opened and closed cupboards getting the coffee fixins, I noticed they were quite bare. As though all he needed to survive was coffee and hooch, not in that order.

"Nice digs. Your parents build this for you?"

"Thanks. No, my father built this for himself so he would not have to drive home when he worked late. Turned out that working late included blondes.

"When mom found out, she put the kibosh on him staying here. It sat empty for a few years, then I decided to move in."

"Parents still married?"

"Yes, Mother's not going to pass up the dough, but she has him on a short leash. Sad about Lila."

"Were you and she an item?"

"We were pretty close. I'm going to miss her." Overhead I heard a door open. I stepped back to look into the loft.

A cream-colored hand set itself on the rail, moving to the spiral stairs. The hand grew into an arm and the arm into a beautiful blond. She stepped on to the stairs and floated down. She seemed to be wearing only a blanket she had wrapped around herself.

"Hi." She giggled when she reached the bottom. She walked over to the couch and pulled a slinky black dress from between the cushions.

"How 'bout you? Are you going to miss Lila Glisan as much as Parker here does?"

"Oh yes. I didn't know her that well, but she was a sweet person." Her face went from happy to sad in an instant. I thought she was going to get all misty. Then she changed back. "But at least now she's in a better place. Bye," she bubbled, bouncing back up the stairs.

She had a point. As long as you consider being in a Chicago overcoat for the rest of eternity better than walking around.

"I guess you couldn't stand to be alone last night? Do you want to change your answer? How well did you know Lila?"

"Look, Lila has, had an image to maintain. We dated a few times to keep her picture in the paper."

"Why would she need to do that?"

"She loved the publicity and the attention. She'd be with me a few times, then somebody else. Always society types."

"Did you bother to get to know her? Or was it only about sex?"

"Whoa. Whoa, it wasn't like that. She stayed here a few times, on the couch. She always got attention even as a kid. She thought she had this image to maintain, but she didn't like the life, not that much anyway." I wasn't talking to the playboy anymore. Ol' Jefferson decided he'd play it straight with me. He had nothing to hide and nothing to prove.

"You're saying everything in the gossip pages was a sham?" I asked, watching him scoop out coffee into his percolator.

"About fifty percent."

"Why don't you try talking into my other ear, you're not making any sense talking into this one." He put the percolator on the stove.

"You play the market?"

"I prefer not to gamble. Bangtails are my game."

"I didn't think so. Let me explain it using horses. You bet on winners right?" I nodded. "You bet on a horse that wins against other good horses. You bet on a horse that's won at Santa Anita, but not on horses that win in some farmer's back forty. Right?" He didn't need to connect any more dots.

"So she wanted to be with rich cat's like you until she got the attention of one she could keep. She have anyone in mind?"

"Not that I know of." I dug the clipping out of my coat pocket, showing it to Jeffy.

"Who's the guy in back?"

"I don't know. He came in before we were leaving. Sally saw him come in. She went over and talked to him. When she came back to the table, she said it was time to go."

"Were you or Lila ready to call it a night?"

"I wasn't and Lila wasn't either, but she didn't argue."

"Who was the ringleader of those two?"

"Neither one was in charge per se, Lila was her own person. She and Sally had been friends a long time. It's funny, she was a very popular person, but she had few friends. Because of that, the friends she did have held a lot of sway over her."

While he was talking, the coffee started percolating. I watched the dark liquid dancing in the globe. Parker pulled a cup out of a cupboard, blew in it and set it down on the counter.

"You were talking about the guy in the clipping."

"Oh, yeah. At the club, the rest of them got in his car. That guy followed us here. I let her out before parking in the underground garage. She went with him and the other two. That was the last time I saw her."

"When was this?"

"A month, month and a half ago."

"How well did you know her friends?"

"Not well. I only saw them in public."

"Sally Kaufman?"

"We went on a few double dates, Lila with me, Sally with whoever she was seeing. For what it's worth she was a true friend of Lila's. They were very close."

"Did Sally ever bring Carl Hanson on one of these dates?"

"No, not as a date. I saw them in public together, but there wasn't anything between them.

"Can you think of anyone who would want her dead?"

"No," he said, shaking his head. I thanked him and walked to the elevator.

When the door opened, I turned back.

"Say, where can a guy get a good steak? Some place you can take a dame to? "

"The Roadhouse. It's on Sprague out in the valley. Good food and not too many people know about it yet. You'll get seated right away."

CHAPTER 17

The Yegg

It was earlier in the day than I usually like to show up at the office. I like to throw a bone to Cap now and then. It makes him feel like he's in charge. I wasn't much in the mood to talk to anyone. I used most of my morning's supply of charm on Jeffy. I figured I would write some overdue reports.

But first, I had to take my car to the motor pool to get the window fixed. They took my old car and gave me another.

The office was too bright, too loud, and too tan. Bureaucracies lack imagination. We tend to dress alike and act alike. We can be very boring, which explains the color of our clothing, furnishings, and office.

I walked around the other desks to mine. On it I found license plate traces of the cars passing Lila's. I would call these people later. Next to the traces I found photos of the thugs who were gunning for me last night. I wanted to work on those things, but first, I wanted to catch up on those reports.

That is one of the wonders of police work that never makes it's way into the movies: report writing. The reason: it's dull and boring. To write a proper report requires talent; not for writing, but for bullshitting. Report writing is more mush-mouth than art.

After an hour of torturing the language on my Underwood, I decided to give Sally a ring. Afterwards, I would pay a visit to Hanson in the lock up, see if he was singing a new tune.

I rang her number. "Good morning. Kaufman residence," said a pleasant sounding woman.

"Good Morning ma'am. This is Detective Hayden with the police department. Is Sally in?"

"Let me see." The phone clunked when she set it down. I counted the keys on the Underwood, 54. I counted again, still 54.

"Hello detective." I've felt warmer arctic winds. I told her so. "What did you expect? Someone murders my best friend. Then you go out and harass and arrest another friend?"

"You mean your boyfriend?" She did not respond. I had to get her talking. "Weren't you and Hanson on a double date with Jefferson Parker and Lila a month ago at Club Cleo?" She didn't take the bait. "Word is you two should have been in a hotel, not a club."

She bit: "How dare you! And what does it matter who I go out in public with?"

"Only matters if one of those people is a murderer. Who is the cat you met at the gin mill that night?" There was some stammering.

"What do you mean?"

"Six foot, dark hair. Greasy looking."

"I, I'm, not sure I know who you mean."

"Don't play that game with me, you know damn well who I mean. The yegg. My buddy Jeff Parker says you spoke with him for quite a while."

"Oh, him. He's a friend from school. I hadn't seen him in years."

"What's his name?"

"He was in town that night. He's, uh, out of town again."

"Where?"

"Somewhere on the east coast. I'm not sure. We didn't talk long."

"Jeff dropped Lila off at his building, where she joined you, Hanson and the mystery date. Now what's his name?" When she didn't answer right away, I continued, "If he's out of town, what's it matter if I know what his name is?"

She started to speak. I broke in, "Before you answer, ask Hanson what happens when you lie to me."

"Vincent Largo," her voice was quieter than cat's feet on carpet. I almost missed it with all the yelling that came from the other side of the room.

"Hayden!" it was Cap.

"Be right there Captain. I've got a very important witness on the phone."

Into the phone I said, "Vincent Largo, why is that name familiar?" She answered with silence. "Sally?"

"Hayden!" Cap bellowed. I looked up. I've seen less enraged bulls at the rodeo. Holding the phone at chest level, I asked, "What?"

"Who is that dead man in the holding cell downstairs?"

"What?" The phone had moved to my waist.

"There's a dead man downstairs! Do you know how much the chief hates it when a prisoner dies in the lock up?" Then it hit me. I finally understood what he was yelling about. I returned the phone to my ear.

"Detective? What's going on? Is Carl OK?"

"I'll have to call you back," I answered, ignoring her protests, and slammed the phone down.

CHAPTER 18

The Dungeon

The lock up is sometimes called O'Malley's Dungeon, after Chief O'Malley. He built it fifteen years ago. And "dungeon" doesn't quite capture the feeling. The station is near the river which divides the city. The lock up is below the basement.

Its depth and closeness to the river made the dungeon a cold, damp, miserable place. Nobody wanted to work the dungeon. Any officer who found himself assigned there knew he had little chance of seeing light again.

Here the brass diverged from bureaucracy tan to battleship grey. Grey walls, grey bars, and grey people. For those reasons (and more) I avoided this place like the clap.

Not only did I have to go to O'Malley's Dungeon, but the suspect I had put down there to shake up was dead.

I checked my gun and the officer let me through two sets of gates. My sunny disposition kept the bulls from talking to me or meeting my gaze.

Three officers were gathered in front of one of the cells. They made hushed comments to one another until I stepped on the floor. All conversation stopped. The cell was open. In it was another officer, and Hanson, who lay on the cot bolted to the floor.

A blanket was at his feet as though it had been flung off him. I reached down feeling his neck for a pulse. I knew I would not find one, his blue fingertips told me so.

I unleashed a string of obscenities that can only come from years on the force and in the Army. And spending my formative years at my old man's knee. Several of the officers blushed and turned away. The desk sergeant jotted notes like a student whose grades were on the line.

I had brought Hanson down here to loosen his lips, not get him killed. I could have done that without any help.

When I finished throwing my fit, I examined Hanson closer. He had a black eye and some bruises on his arms and body. It looked like he had been in a fight.

"You find him?" I asked the officer in the cell with me.

"Yes detective. His blanket was up like he was asleep and had been that way since I came on at eight. We sent the others to the jail about an hour later. Course, we left him where he was because we didn't have any reports on him. We didn't know what you wanted done with him.

"I decided to check on him. You know, see if he wanted some coffee or something. I pulled down the blanket and there he was, dead."

"You don't make rounds? You don't check to make sure everyone is OK?"

"Like I said, I thought he was asleep."

"Don't get your feathers all ruffled detective, things like this happen." The plump desk sergeant had come over, standing before the cell. He had tucked a toothpick in one corner of his mouth. It bobbed around when he spoke. I walked over staring down at his fat face.

"Do they sergeant? Do healthy people take the big sleep for no reason?"

He plucked the toothpick from his mouth, using it to punctuate his words as he spoke. "They do if you beat them hard enough. But don't you worry none. We'll take care of this nice and quiet like." He winked at me while returning his toothpick to his mouth.

"I could see where that would be the case sergeant, if I had wanted him dead. You see, he was the star suspect in a star murder. So why would I kill my own best suspect?" I removed the toothpick from his mouth and flicked it at his face. It bounced off his eyebrow, landing on the floor.

"Whatever beating he took, he took it in here. What kind of shit hole are you running here?"

He reached up and felt his eyebrow. Pulling his hand away, he stared at it as if he were afraid he'd find gray matter.

"It didn't happen on my watch."

"Why don't you crawl back over to your desk and stack pencils so a real cop can do his job. Is that Jake with you sarge?"

"Oh, you think you're better than us? You think you don't need our help?"

"No, it's because you are the cock of the walk in a shit-hole. These young guys made a mistake which they're atoning for. Some day they'll be free of this place. What about you sarge? Why are you here? Why are you going be here until you put your papers in?" I asked, keeping my voice level. I gave him the once over, noticing small veins around his nose.

"Did you bust some brass' girlfriend? No, that sounds too much like work. Oh, I know." I reached up, pinching his nose between my index and middle finger. I drug him along as I walked through the dungeon.

"Where's your stash sarge? Is it in your desk? Or are you still trying to hide it? You're still trying to hide it, although, I'm sure all your guys must know about it." He protested and tried to free his nose. I clamped down harder. "What the hell are you doing? You can't do this." His voice came out like munchkin.

"Let's see. Where would a lazy-assed drunk like you, keep his bottle?" I looked to the ceiling. I saw pipes. "Is it up there? Na, you couldn't get your fat ass up there."

His men had gathered around. I saw shocked faces, but none of them held much sympathy, some even had the makings of a smile. I saw a one-hole latrine off to one side.

"Is it in here? Come on, let's go see." In the head I lifted the lid off the tank. Inside was a bottle of hooch. I lifted it out, holding it in front of his face.

"Here it is, in the poor man's icebox."

I let go of his nose. He lunged for the bottle. I put my hand on his face, shoving him backward. He stumbled into the corner and slid down the wall. He sat there, defeated. He didn't even protest when I poured the whiskey down the drain.

"There you go sarge." I dropped the dead soldier in his lap on my way out closing the door so he could cry in private.

CHAPTER 19

Internal Affairs

Some things in this life grate on my nerves. Mornings and report writing. But I'm also not fond of drunkards, especially when they are on duty. I hate the dungeon. And I hate crooked cops.

A saint I ain't, but I'm not on the take. And I don't set anyone up, either to frame them or free them. For one bright shiny moment the sergeant was all those things. He was a lush. He was the slimy filth of the grey dungeon. He was the dumb flattie who looks the other way when the corner store gets knocked over. So long as someone lines his pockets.

Sarge, in his infinite stupidity had managed to push all my buttons; I pushed some of his.

With sarge tucked away in the think tank, I could get to work.

The blue birds were staring at me like a room full of twenty year-old virgins told they were going to get laid. Shocked disbelief and hope lined the faces of these men.

"Detective, I can't believe you did that. He's a pretty good guy and he doesn't always drink," said one of the younger bulls.

"You wouldn't think that if he were lit and a riot broke out down here. Why don't you go join him?" He shook his head. "Good. Now shut your hole."

"With all due respect detective, who the hell do you think you are? You come in here yelling at everyone without cause. Sgt. Dekum offers to help and you dump him in the toilet. We're supposed to kiss your ass?" This was from an officer leaning against the wall, arms crossed. I had missed him before, I don't know how: he matched me in height and weight: six foot, about 230.

"Don't kiss my ass, I don't drop my pants for any man. Your Sgt. Dekum is worthless and I needed to get him out of the way before he FUBARed my case."

"Didn't you FUBAR your own case when you beat that guy to death?" he nodded his head down the hall to Hanson's cell. I advanced toward him. He stood away from the wall.

"I didn't touch him. Could be one of the other hoods down here did it. If you slack-jawed jaspers had done your jobs, he'd be alive." His jaw flexed.

"If you're trying to get me to take a poke at you, it's not going to work. I ain't going to do it. I'm not a fool. I know I'm at the end of the line. If I hit you then I'm off this train. I can't afford that." Our eyes burned into each other from a foot away. "Well, you've got our attention. What do you want us to do?"

"What have you guys done?"

"Nothing. Sgt. Dekum didn't know how you wanted it handled. So we called looking for you before we did anything," answered the bull who found Hanson. "Should I call a doctor?"

"Yes, you should start there." I called Burkholter's office. The old man wasn't in, but they were sending someone over. Next, I called Internal Affairs.

Nobody was happy after that.

IA grilled everybody; me, the officers, Dekum. If they were curious about why he was in the latrine, they chose not to ask. Even they were smart enough to realize that was the least of our problems. They also called in the officers who had worked the last shift. Nobody would fess to anything.

Davison showed up from the coroner's office. He could not determine the cause of death and was not willing to guess until an autopsy.

IA wanted to know why I put Hanson in the dungeon instead of the county caboose. I told them it was all in my report. If they wanted to, they could read it.

"Why don't you explain it to us?" one of them asked.

"Why didn't you pay more attention in school? Does your wife have to read the morning paper to you?"

"There's no need to get upset. I want to hear it in your own words."

"My own words? Who do you suppose wrote the damn thing, your wife? Actually, I tried to get her to do it, but I kept her busy with other things last night." For the second time that morning another cop wanted to hit me.

"You're not making this easy on yourself."

"I've done nothing wrong. If you remembered what it was like to be a real cop, you'd be trying to figure out who did this instead of busting my balls. "

"I'm trying to figure out what happened here. If you were more help- ful, we could get out of here sooner."

"What were you doing the night before last? Did you spend it with your family? That's lovely. That's ducky. You want to know what I was doing? I was awakened and called to a murder scene. The girl was very beautiful until her guts spilled, while she was still alive. It was very ugly. Heart over there, lungs on either side. Everything was on display as though she needed a good airing out.

"Last night I got a Tommy gun wake up call. A chopper squad paid me a visit and tried to air me and my dame out. I aced them right there.

"These last two evenings have not been good for me. People seem in- tent on waking me and keeping me from getting a good night's sleep, leaving me irritable. So, do whatever you need to do to me, to make yourself feel good about your pathetic snitch life. Take away my birth- day if you can, you stupid gink."

Like I said, I hate crooked cops, but I also hate snitches. It seems con- tradictory; how do you catch crooked cops, without IA? Maybe a trip to the parking lot was all you needed.

He finally got tired of me berating him. And I got tired of berating him. I left but they warned me that they may want to talk to me again. Yippie.

I got back to my office at a quarter after noon. I needed to call Nora.

"What happened to you? I was beginning to think that you had found another woman."

'"Hanson died."

"That's awful. What happened?"

"We don't know yet. Look, I don't want to talk about that right now. I did manage to find an up-scale chow house for this evening."

"Oh? What is it? Have I heard of it before?"

"Don't think so. It's a new place." While talking to Nora, I watched a guy come in the office. He wore a gray linen suit. His nervous hands worked the brim of his brown lid.

"So should I go buy a flak jacket or are you going to do a better job of keeping the baddies away?"

"Buy the flak jacket. I like my women to weigh 200 pounds." The guy searched the room, his eyes wide open.

"Then you wouldn't mind if I ordered two sixteen ounce steaks, to help me get to the 200 hundred pound mark?" The guy caught the eye of one of the other detectives. They were speaking.

"Sure, then I can hide behind you when the baddies start firing. Listen doll, I got to go. See you about 6:30? OK, bye." The other detective pointed the guy to me.

"Detective Hayden?"

"Yeah." He stuck his hand out. I shook it.

"George Fox. Are you working the Lila Glisan murder? Well, I saw something I should tell you about."

CHAPTER 20

George Fox

I indicated a chair next to my desk, then took my own. Fox took his hat off his head.

Fox was shorter and slimmer than me by a few inches. His had a pudgy baby face, but he was not fat. Large eyes cased the room like the bogeyman might jump from under a desk and Fox would have to make a quick escape.

"See anything you like?"

"What? Oh, it's that I've never been in a police station before."

"Is it everything you hoped and dreamed it would be?"

"Huh? Oh, it's nice. I thought I would see jail cells or something."

"We've got them everywhere: downstairs, in the heads, the chiefs office. But for some reason, they overlooked this room. You don't want to be near one anyway, people seem to be dying in them."

He remained wide eyed, looking over the room.

"You know something about Lila's murder?"

"Uh, what?" I seemed to have confused Fox. "Oh, yeah, well . . ." His hands were in his lap. They continued to wear out the brim of his hat.

"Whenever you are ready there George." While Shakespeare collected his thoughts, I dug through the things on my desk. There was the notice to Lila's funeral, the guest list from old Cormack's party, and the license plate tracings.

"Did you know Lila?"

"N-no." His right hand left the brim of his hat to run through his hair. I sat back in my chair, taking in Fox.

"I'm sure there is something you want to say or you wouldn't be here. If it has to do with Lila's murder, you should speak up. Her father loved her very much and would like to see justice done." He hung his hat from his knee and held his head in both hands.

"I knew Lila a long time. Well, I didn't know her, I only spoke to her a couple of times. I met her in college. In the spring of my junior year we had an English class together. I spoke to her a few times in class. Things like how she did on the test. If she finished the homework. What she thought of the professor, those sorts of things.

"I knew who she was of course. I guess that intimidated me. If she had been anyone else, I would have asked her out. As it was, I knew what caliber men she dated and I was not it."

"How was she to talk to? Polite? Rude?"

"She was great to talk to, very polite. I was generally a good student. I got good grades and made it to class on time, that sort of thing. There wasn't a class in the lecture hall before ours. I got to the hall early so I could talk to her."

"Let me guess, she was always to class on time and turned in perfect papers."

"Yeah," his brows knitted together. "How did you know?"

"I spent several hours in her house. You could have eaten out of the fireplace. There was a big stain on the living room rug. I managed to get it out though."

Fox had an assortment of confused looks. He paraded one out for me. I have to admit he was a master.

"You were telling me about your romantic rendezvous with Lila."

He cleared his throat and rubbed the underside of his nose with the backside of his index finger. "Well," he said clearing his throat again, a red flush crawled up his face. "That's a bit of an exaggeration. You might have guessed that I'm not much of, um, uh, a ladies man."

I couldn't bring myself to lay the heavy artillery on him. I felt bad for Fox. Here was a guy who had an opportunity that most guys would have killed for and he was too shy to even ask.

"What do you do?" I asked, leaning back in my chair.

"What? I-I'm sorry."

"For a living. You took an English class in your junior year of college. That's not something an accountant or other number jockey would do. You're not a salesman or journalist as shy as you are. Your suit is nice, but not great, so you're not a paper filer. So, what do you do?"

"I'm not sure what this has to do with anything, but I'm in advertising. My dad owns the firm. I majored in business, and minored in English." I stared at him for a few moments. He took his hat off his knee and began worrying the brim again.

"Advertising, and your father owns the business. Is there a lot of kale in that?"

He blinked several times, thinking it over. "We do pretty good. Not like Lila's father, but we make out."

"She may have gone out with you. She wouldn't have married you. Nothing to do with you, she didn't know what the hell she wanted. In a year or two she would have married whomever she was dating. That would've lasted eighteen months. Then she'd go look for someone else. A man much like her dad who had made all the major decisions in her life."

We sat staring at each other. Me wondering why I would bother to tell him such a thing. He was wondering how much more of this he was going to have to put up with.

The two of us sat silent. Around us detectives banged out new versions of Dick and Jane on their typewriters.

"You want some water?" I asked.

"Uh, sure." I remained in my chair for a few seconds before walking to the water cooler. I filled the cups. Emptied mine, refilled it.

"Here you go," I said handing him the paper cup. I resumed my position.

"So, what about Lila?"

"Well," he cleared his throat, "so, I thought about her all that summer. In the fall I tried to get classes with her again. I couldn't find out what she was taking. About halfway through the quarter, I saw her in the quad with friends. I didn't want to bother her while she was with her friends so I followed her back to her dorm."

I had been looking at the stuff on my desk wondering how much longer this was going to take. I was hungry. Now, I looked back up; he had my attention again. His steady eyes looked in mine.

"I guess that's how it began. I wanted to talk to her, but she was always with friends. There was no way I could speak to her while her friends were around. Before I knew it, I was following her. I followed her to her classes. I followed her when she came home. I followed her on dates. We went to some nice restaurants and clubs. Sometimes I couldn't afford to eat at the restaurant, so I'd wait outside."

"You weren't actually spending time with her."

"No, but somehow, that took the place of dating her. I realized that I could not compete with the guys she was dating. They were so much better looking than me. They could afford to take her to the places where I couldn't even afford to order a salad."

"You're lucky she didn't spot your tail. Her old man could have arranged for a copper squad to put the hurt on you."

"I know what you're thinking detective. You're thinking I'm some sort of, uh" he cleared his throat, "nut job or something."

"Oh no. It's all reasonable. I'm currently spying on three dames. Sometimes it's fun to put on my old fatigues and sneak up on them. And sometimes, I put on some face paint like we used in the war. I sneak up as close as I can and jump from the bushes, screaming as loud as I can. It's a great way to scare the crap out of them and to get their large boyfriend to paste you in the kisser. In fact, I'm late to catch one of them in the shower." I started to push myself out of my chair.

"No, wait. I assure you, there is a point to this." He had reached out, putting a hand on my forearm. "I'm not proud of this, but I had to tell you that so you will understand what I say next."

I sat back down. "OK, but it better come fast."

"Well, um, she began to spend more and more time with a group of people."

"Sally Kaufman, Nancy Mason, Carl Hanson and Vincent Largo."

"She had been friends with Sally and Nancy. I remember Carl. I don't remember that last name, Vincent, um . . ."

"Largo." I pulled the clipping form an inside pocket of my suit coat. "Yes, the guy with the goatee. I may have seen the guy in back, but I can't be sure. I don't know the guy in front with Lila."

"These others, were they students?"

"I'm not sure."

"If you have a yearbook you could find them in there."

"Yeah, I hadn't thought of that." He sat back, trying to pick up his story. "So they—she and these other people—went out as a group. Lila even stopped dating. After about two weeks of this, I began to think about the very thing that you mentioned. One of these guys would see me and beat me up or something.

"One night I watched them go in a club together. I made up my mind to give it up and go home. As I reached for the starter, someone yanked my door open and drug me out of the car. These three guys took me to an alley. They wanted to know why I had been following Lila and her friends. When I told them I didn't know what they were talking about, one of them punched me in the stomach.

"I had never been in a fight before, and the pain was very surprising. I doubled over. Between tears and gasps I told them what they wanted to know." His hands shook as he told his story. Fox tried to hide it by holding his hands together in his lap.

"By the time I caught my breath, I was able to stand up again. The guy who seemed to be the leader leaned close, our noses were almost touching. He said: 'You stop hanging around or you'll get more of this, capish?' I remember that his breath smelled like peppermint.

"I nodded and everything went black. One of them must have hit me with a sap or something. I came to sometime later. My head was throbbing and I had a big lump behind my ear. My wallet and things were lying on the ground. It took me a while to pick everything up and make it to my car."

"Did you report it?"

"I'm sure you have figured out that I am not a brave man. I thought the best thing would be to leave it all alone."

"Were they upset that you were following Lila or the group?"

"At first I thought it was Lila. Now I know it was the group." Fox stopped all his hand wringing and hat mauling and the other hinky things he had been doing. "Rose and Thistle." The words passed through his lips like a hot August Chinook over a wheat field in the Palouse. When the wheat is dry and ready to cut, the wind brushes it together making faint rustling sounds.

"What? Give me a sign here, I'm not sure what you mean."

"You wouldn't know about it unless you've been to the university. Even if you had been to university, you may not have heard of it. It's, uh," Fox swallowed again, "a secret club."

"Like a fraternity or sorority?"

"No. I don't know anything about it, except that they, um, guard their secrecy. Only the best people get in and they form some eternal bond or something."

"What? Never mind. What does this have to do with Lila?"

"That's it. That's what I'm talking about. According to rumors, once you're in, you can't get out." We stared at each other. I no longer heard the typing and ringing and talking. "If Lila wanted out, she would have to die."

CHAPTER 21

Chief Hewitt

I didn't know what to make of Fox or his story. One thing I did know, I was damn hungry. I told Fox I wanted him to look over his yearbooks to find people who were in Lila's group. I also had him eye the shots of the goons who tried to put me under the night before; he didn't recognize them. Finished, I arranged to meet him tomorrow.

I had a little field trip planned for after lunch—I was going to the university. Gathering things up from my desk, I looked over the list of license traces. I was not surprised to see that Fox had passed Lila's twice.

Fox seemed to be an excitable little guy. He was something of a mystery.

Murder is easy to understand; the motive is usually jealousy, rage, or pay-off.

Those are understandable, not agreeable, but understandable.

I can't get savvy with the idea of tailing some skirt because you're too shy to talk to her. I figured he was on the square; who would want to admit to such a thing if it weren't true?

All these things passed through my mind on the way to Frank's.

"How's Nora?" Frank asked, smiling.

"She's silk. I wish this case was." I took my usual seat at the bar.

"I guess you know how to show her a good time." He tossed a newspaper in front of me. It was opened to a small story about the shooting.

"If you buddied around with me, I could tell you my secrets about dames. For instance, did you know they like it when you sneak after them and hide in bushes?"

"I haven't heard of that one."

"It seems to work for some guys." I ordered and thirty minutes later I tipped Frank and headed down to the university.

Downing University is in the tiny town of Duncan. The campus and city was a sea of green and splotches of color as flowers made themselves known. It was a nice change from the washed out shades I had become accustomed to living in the city.

Downing was not the largest university in the west, but it was the most prestigious.

The Duncan police station was easy to find. The town was so small, everything was easy to find. The main street was home to a gas station, the post office, a small grocery store, city hall and the police station. On the tree-lined side streets, were houses (some with signs advertising for boarders). Down one street I saw buildings that appeared to house both the grade and high schools.

Across that street was a large park.

The station was a small two-story affair. Patrol officers used the bottom floor. Admin and Detectives used the upper floor.

The main floor was an open area with a counter separating the public from the officers. A uniformed officer greeted me at the counter.

"What can I do for you sir?"

"Here on business." I showed him my shield and ticket. "I wanted to let you know I was here and ask Chief Hewitt some questions." I had called city hall to get the chief's name; that's the personal touch I provide.

"Can I let the chief know why you're here?" A subtle, but noticeable change came over him. Cops tend to dislike cops from another department sniffing over their turf. The best way to diffuse the problem is to ask them for help. Offering help, without an invitation causes them to get cocky.

"I'm here about the murder of Senator Glisan's daughter. I doubt it has anything to do with Duncan, I know that she went to school over at Downing. I thought I could track down some of her friends who used to go there." It also helps to drop the name of a powerful senator who has a building at Downing named after him. The only reason for Duncan's existence was the university, and the town's residents knew it.

"Let me call the chief, see if he's in."

Less than a minute later I was pressing the flesh with Chief Hewitt.

The last time the chief was in foot pursuit of a crook was when a bully had stolen his lunch money on the playground. His crisp blue uniform curved over his large gut. Brass stars decorated his collar. His second chin hid the knot of his tie.

Hewitt showed me a chair across from his desk. He asked, "So, you're here because the murder of Judge Glisan's daughter?" He must not have heard of Glisan's promotion from the bench.

"I drew the short straw on that. What do you know about Rose and Thistle?" The void of space could not have been more quiet than the void between us at that moment.

"I'm not sure I know what you mean."

"Have you ever met Senator Glisan?"

"I have been in his courtroom."

"So you have an idea of what kind of man he is. He draws a lot of water in this state. He wants his daughter's killer brought to justice. James and I drink out of the same bottle. If I were to tell him that you wouldn't help me, he's liable to get upset."

He thought it over for a moment. "There's not much to tell. It's a group of college students who sit around talking about how to make the world a better place. Philosophy, that sort of thing."

"College kids kicking around Plato? Come on Chief. Lila died because of something to do with Rose and Thistle. I heard that they take some sort of blood oath. That doesn't sound like college kids sitting around chinning on world peace."

"Look, I don't know who you've been talking to, but I'm sure most of it is a lie. The group exists. They have regular meetings like the Elks and the Masons and even the Grange. They don't do anything like what's said about them.

"People in small towns know everything about their neighbors. Sometimes when they don't know anything about a neighbor, they make up things to fill in the blanks. Rose and Thistle is secretive. That makes people talk even more."

"Well, if it's no big deal, you can tell me who their Grand Poobah is, and I'll get out of your hair." Again, I suffered through the silence of the void. He rocked forward in his leather chair. He clasped his hands together on his desktop around his considerable gut.

"That's the problem with these college organizations, I'm not a student so I wouldn't know."

"You must have some idea."

"None. If there's nothing—"

"Does the school have its own security or do they depend on you?"

"My jurisdiction includes Downing University. But I assure you, there's nothing else to find out."

"I'm sure you won't mind then if I do some snooping of my own?"

He sat back again, spreading his arms. "Be my guest."

CHAPTER 22

Downing University

I thought of tracking down Downing's president, but I'd never get the straight dope from him. He's from the same cloth as Chief Hewitt. No matter how fast I was, I couldn't out run Ma Bell; no doubt, the chief was on the blower the second I closed the door.

By now they had a game plan. The president knew what Chief Lardbottom told me. He wouldn't give me any more information than that. When the president got off the phone, he'd brief the rest of the admin staff. No matter who I talked to, I'd get the same story.

All this trouble for little ol' me. I didn't buy everything Fox had to say about this club. Outside of the mob, who would off someone for leaving their group? With the song and dance Fox gave and the Chief's one man Mutt and Jeff routine, something was up. I didn't feel like playing any games, at least none of theirs.

I found a spot under a maple tree next to the road to park my car. I had never been to Downing before. I'd never felt like lowering the snootiness quotient of the university before.

After making my way around a few buildings and trees, I found myself in the quad. It was about three acres of grass, trees and flowers beds that I'm sure would have impressed somebody. I've never considered flowers much of a threat so I rarely notice them.

This late in the day, few students were walking around the campus. A few were playing a pick-up game of cricket to one side of a little mound in the center of the quad. Others were losing themselves in books and homework. Some were enjoying the warm spring sun.

Choosing my victim at random, I stopped in front of a girl reading an Agatha Christie novel.

"The frog with the outrageous accent did it."

Her eyes popped up over the edge of her book. I got the idea that she was looking down her nose at me. Neat trick as I was standing and she was sitting on the ground, her skirt gathered around her legs.

"Poirot is Belgian."

"Is there a difference? I've been to both of them. I'm not sure there's a difference." She gave me the kind of sigh she would give the help if they had put two salad forks in front of her at dinner. "What do you know about Rose and Thistle?"

"What?" she asked, annoyed at having to speak to the likes of me.

"Rose and Thistle. They are some sort of club here. Know anything about them?"

"No. Should I?"

Ten yards away, a cat in an oxford shirt, chinos and a white sweater over his shoulders sat on a blanket, reading.

"How 'bout you Biff? You know anything about Rose and Thistle?" I asked from where I stood. A few heads turned.

"I haven't the foggiest idea what you're talking about . . . officer." A smug smile crawled over his face. His voice carried the arrogance of a man who has figured the surprise ending of a movie halfway through.

I tipped my hat back on my head, scratching at the hairline.

"Congratulations. You made me. I guess next time, I'll dress like a tennis jerk." Fifteen yards away, a group of students were talking and giving me the eye.

Walking toward them, I called out. "Hey, young aristocrats, you know anything about Rose and Thistle?" They looked aghast at the barbarian who dare trod on their sacred grass. A few shook their heads.

I raised my voice as I passed from one group to the next. I now had the attention of most of the people in the quad. It was time to round up the stragglers.

I was now forty yards from the cricket players. I yelled across the distance: "Hey, jocks, you know anything about Rose and Thistle?" I turned and yelled the other direction: "Rose and Thistle! Ollie, Ollie oxen free. Come out, come out wherever you are."

Everyone in and around the quad was now staring at the barbarian. It wasn't my best work. If I had tried to play it by the book, I'd be in the president's office dancing the same dance I did with the chief. At least this way I was getting fresh air.

I had everyone's attention here. They knew I was looking for information about a club that may or may not be dangerous. If anyone here knew anything, word would get to the right people. It was time to move through the campus spreading my words of annoyance.

I walked along a cement path away from the quad. I asked everyone in shouting range if they knew anything about Rose and Thistle.

There was movement on my right. A face peeked at me from behind a tree. She had been in the quad near the tennis player.

"You shouldn't be calling for them," she said in hushed tones.

"Why? Are they going to yammer at me about Plato's dialogues?" She looked at me like she didn't know what I was talking about; I get that a lot. "Are you a cop?" she pressed on after glancing around. By now, most had lost interest in me, except the squirrels with their incessant chattering. "Yeah. I'm investigating the death of Lila Glisan. She's the daughter of the esteemed Senator Judge Glisan."

"So you're not local?"

"No. Though, my mother said I was on several occasions. Oh, I thought you said 'loco.'" Now she gave me a disapproving frown. I seemed to get a lot of that too, most of the time from women.

She looked around again. "It's not safe to talk here. Meet me at the library in ten minutes. I'll be in periodicals." That's how I knew I was at Downing. Everyone I know calls them magazines.

She gave me directions to the library then scampered off in the other direction.

June Kayer

The ivy covered brick walls of the library used three floors to reach for the sky. The builders should have tried a little harder.

To reach the entrance, I climbed a set of stone steps guarded by a pair of stone lions. The interior was a mix of the foyer of Jefferson's building and Senator Judge Glisan's office. Marble, wood, solemnity, and class. Dark stained oak bookcases lined the walls and formed aisles. Marble columns supported the ceiling.

At the reference desk, I asked a librarian where the magazines were. She pointed, I followed.

I was reading a magazine article about Ronald Reagan's latest movie. That guy needed to find another job because his acting was going nowhere. The woman walked over. When she saw me, she glommed around the library.

The magazine area was more open than the rest of the library. There were few columns, no bookcases to block the view and tables to sit around.

Without a tree in the way, I was able to see her for the first time.

She wore a white spring dress with a blue floral pattern. Light brown hair down to her shoulders. Blue eyes. A beer or two and she'd look like Donna Reed.

We moved to a table where we could both glom over the room.

"Alright, what's your story?"

"Can I see your badge first?" I fished the case out of my coat flopping it on the table. She looked at the black leather case, to me and then back to the case.

Her hands grabbed it. Opening it, she stared at the tin, tracing her fingers over its outlines. Then she looked at the ticket comparing the photo to the genuine article. Done, she closed it up and placed the case where I had tossed it.

"I read about Lila's death in the paper. It's hard to believe. I was a sophomore her senior year. A lot of rich kids come here to Downing, but none of them quite as famous as Lila. She's not a big celebrity like they have in Hollywood, but she was our celebrity." She stopped and raked her teeth over her lower lip. She was beyond crying. She looked like she had, but now she was in control.

I took my buzzer and put it back in my coat. "What's your name?"

"June Kayer."

"What do you know about Rose and Thistle?"

"Do you think they did this?"

"I don't even know who they are. At this point, anything you know would be helpful."

"There's not much to know unless you are in the club. Most people who go here never even hear the name. Members join in their senior year. Only those with money, power or a family connection to the club can join."

"Into what? What does the club do? I didn't see a lodge while driving through town."

"It's not like those other clubs. Rose and Thistle try to gain and maintain power. Members include politicians, the wealthy, leaders of industry. Anyone who can help them achieve their goals."

"What are those goals?"

"I'm not sure." While we spoke, her eyes held mine. Now she glanced over the room. She looked at me again.

"How did Lila get in, wealth, power or connection?"

"It's not connection; her father didn't go to school here. Only people who graduated from Downing can join. That doesn't stop them from getting outside people to do jobs for them."

"Has the senator done anything for the club?"

"Not that I can find. I've checked his record both as a judge and senator, and everything seems above board." It was my turn to get a slant of the room. I did it to buy time, to give my mind a chance to work this idea over.

"I've heard that once you're in, you're in for life. Anything to that?" I asked.

"I've also heard that."

"Who belongs?"

She sat back and straightened out the skirt of her dress. "I don't know. There are no lists that I have seen and no one member seems to know all the others. "

"So how do they know each other? Is there a secret handshake, a nod and a wink, what?"

"I don't know how their organization works. The seniors who join, only know each other and their recruiters. As they rise in the ranks of the society, they meet more people and learn more of the objectives. In the beginning they learn a pair of phrases to identify each other."

"A sign and counter-sign?"

"I guess. They use two Latin phrases. The first is: facta non verba. The second, the counter-sign, is: ad nocendum potentes. 'Deeds not words' and 'we have the power to harm."

"How do you know so much about them?"

"I'm studying journalism and on the school newspaper. I was going to write a story about them. My investigating must have roused some suspicions.

"I live on campus. My roommate was on suspension at the start of the year and flunked out last quarter. The school didn't replace her, so I've had the dorm room all to myself. A few days before I was to submit the story, I came home to find my room ransacked. I had left the story on my desk next to my typewriter. The story was gone. Someone had typed a note and left it in the typewriter."

From her purse Jane pulled out a folded sheet of typing paper. She handed it to me. Her eyes held a plea, for what, I didn't know. I took the paper, unfolding it.

In the center of the page was the message: We have the power to harm.

"Did you go to the police?"

"No, I didn't. They wouldn't have done anything anyway."

"You don't know that."

"My dad was a cop. Don't be so surprised. He started saving money for my education early. It was his dream that I go to school, get an education. Get a good job.

"He used to tell me about his job. He wanted to scare me away. I guess he did, but I learned a lot from him. I learned enough to recognize a good cop when I see one. I interviewed Chief Hewitt for my story. That's when I realized he wasn't a good cop. He tried to convince me that Rose and Thistle did not exist."

"I've heard the same speech."

"When I saw you in the quad, I knew that you would do something."

"Where's your old man work?"

"Portland. He died last year. He was first to arrive at a grocery store robbery. He pulled up as the crook was leaving." A single tear formed in her eye. She didn't wipe it away. Another did not follow. "He could have put his papers in two years ago. He was going to retire when I finished school. He wanted to make sure there was enough money for me to get through school."

"I'm sorry to hear that Miss Kayer. Is the force taking care of you and your mother?"

"Yes. Full pension and he had a life insurance policy. I should drop it after what Rose and Thistle did, but because of my father, I had to tell you what I know."

I sat back in the chair. Something didn't add up. "Chased off? All they did was wreck your room and write a nasty note."

Her eyes looked into mine and did not waver as she said, "That's not all they left. I found a goat's head on my desk."

CHAPTER 24

Nancy Mason

An hour is not a long time. In the time since the start of man an hour is a drop in the ocean. In a man's lifetime we lose an hour among the days, months and years. When you have nothing to do but think unpleasant thoughts, that hour stretches and grows. The fence posts along the road crawl past no matter how hard you press on the accelerator. It's impossible to outrun those thoughts in your head.

What was Lila doing mixed up with this bunch? From what I knew about her, she didn't want power. She wanted to marry well. Her goal was to find a husband and have some fun along the way. How much power would she need for such simple goals? Unless that's where she was planning to find her husband.

I didn't want to believe all that I had heard about Rose and Thistle.

Hell, I didn't want to believe they were real in the first place, let alone that they were a gruesome bunch of rich kids. All I had to track them down was a sign and counter-sign. And the knowledge that only graduates of Downing could be a member.

Back in the city limits I stopped at the first payphone I found. Nancy Mason was not home, but her roommate was happy to tell me where she was.

Talbot & Hunt was an upscale department store downtown. It had started here and had spread. There were now stores in Portland and Seattle. Mason worked at the women's accessories counter.

I looked out of place there among all the women's finery. Hell, in my rumpled suit, I'd look out of place in the haberdashery (damn, I'd been at Downing too long). Even the house detective was better dressed than I was.

I stood back out of sight until she finished with the customer she was helping. I didn't want to give her time to think about why I was there.

She was looking at something under the counter. "Facta non verba," I said to the top of her head. Her head popped up, her eyes showing whites around the iris. When she recognized me, she got even more nervous.

"Detective, what are you doing here?" Her eyes darted about, looking for someone, anyone to rescue her.

"That's not the right counter-sign. Let's try again. Facta non verba." Her eyes returned to my mine. Fear was in her eyes.

"You should be careful with that. If the wrong person heard, you would be in trouble."

"You ever kill a kraut with your Ka-Bar buried in his gut and his head in your hand? You watch the life drain from his eyes as his blood pumps out on your hand. No? Then let me worry about how much trouble can I get into. I'm a big boy now.

"Is there someplace we can talk where you can focus on me instead of every shadow that passes by?"

"Yeah, hold on." She called to a woman working on a display some distance away, telling her that she was taking a break.

I followed her through a storeroom to a small office. A cheap wooden desk sat in one corner against the wall. Besides the desk, the room held a pair of chairs, a file cabinet and a couple of clothing racks.

"How did you find out?"

"Some little birds told me. Was Lila killed because she wanted out?"

"That and she was threatening to tell her father." That explained her tongue or lack of.

"Who did it? Carl?"

"I don't know. It wasn't Carl though. He was with us at the party."

"Was Carl in the club?"

"Yes, he was our mentor. He recruited us, took us to the meetings and such."

"Would you recognize anyone from these meetings?"

"I never saw anybody, well, not their faces. Everybody wears robes and masks. The only people I knew by sight was Lila, Sally and Carl."

"Masks like the Lone Ranger?"

"No, they covered the whole face. They wore colored robes to show the wearer's rank. We are new, so we wear white robes."

"What about Vincent Largo?"

"I never talked to him. He was Carl's overseer. He'd show up once in a while when we were out."

"Sally spoke with him." It was a statement not a question and she knew it.

"Sally likes being in Rose and Thistle. As we all did in the beginning. It was fun being part of a big secret like that. But Sally likes it. She sees it as her chance to be somebody. She talked to Vincent whenever he was around."

"What did you talk about at these meetings?"

"Nothing. They were like classes to teach us and how to perform the rituals. We have rituals for everything. For the opening and closing of meetings, for initiation, for everything. They don't discuss business with initiates."

"Where were these meetings held?"

"I don't know, we were always blindfolded when Carl drove us to them." It figured. Nothing in this case was going to be easy. I sat back rubbing my upturned face with my hands.

"How did you get in?"

"They approached Lila and Sally when I wasn't around. Then, they had no idea what joining would mean. They knew only rich and powerful people could join. Sally wanted to and Lila didn't. Lila didn't care about power. She only cared about money in that it could buy her the things she wanted, but she didn't care about being rich.

"Lila said she would join only if they admitted me. She didn't think they would allow me in, she figured she was safe. Somehow, Sally convinced Carl and Carl convinced the elders."

"Were there many women?"

"Carl said there weren't many."

"Does Senator Glisan know about Rose and Thistle?"

"I don't know. Lila was getting tired of the whole thing. She was like that. She got interested in something for a while, then would get bored with it. She tried to learn the flute once. And she wrote poetry for a short time. She gave up French after a week.

"I wasn't surprised when she told me she wanted out. They had told us that we were in for life, but nobody believed it. She had been arguing with Carl about it for a month. He kept telling her she couldn't quit. She tried to stay away from him. She tried to go on more dates alone and that sort of thing.

"He started showing up on her dates. Last week, she and Carl had a big argument. We (Carl, Sally, Lila and I) all went to dinner. Everyone was a little tense because Carl and Lila were not getting along as you can imagine. She told him that she was going to quit. She was going to tell her father when he got back in town and he would bring the government down on them.

"I knew she was serious. She didn't mention her father often. When she did, she meant it. Carl knew it too. He got up from dinner and stormed out. That was the last time I saw them together."

"How did Lila and her father get along?"

"They loved each other. When he was in town, we ate dinner with him all the time. He's a very nice man."

"Why did Lila get a house of her own then?"

"She wanted some independence. She wanted people to respect her. Everyone said her father took care of everything for her."

"It's hard to disprove that when daddy pays all the bills. Did Carl's actions leading up to the murder give you any clue about what would happen?"

"No. I know you don't like him, but he is nice enough."

"The truth is, I didn't like him." I watched her waiting for the words to sink in.

"What? Didn't? What changed that you like him now."

"He's dead for one thing." I told her how I arrested him and that he died in his cell.

I've seen plaster that had more color in it than Nancy's face had when I told her what happened. Her eyes widened again. Her hands shook in her lap.

"Do you realize what this means? They killed him. They were afraid that he would tell you everything and they killed him." She stood up. "You have to leave now. I shouldn't have told you anything. God, I hope they didn't see me talking to you." I stood up and put my hands on her shoulders to calm her.

"Look, there's no way they could have gotten to Carl. I wasn't followed. Nobody knows I spoke with you." The shaking stopped, but she was still scared.

"You have to get out of here."

"OK, I'm done anyway. Is there a way I can leave without anyone seeing me?" She pointed me to the back exit, and I left.

CHAPTER 25

The Roadhouse

I had enough of Lila and her strange friends for one evening. I didn't want to think about the case anymore, Unfortunately, I couldn't take my mind off it. This case was hinky from the start and nothing I'd learned along the way had made it any less hinky.

It's odd to know the motive of the crime before I have a good suspect. I knew there was a connection between Vincent Largo and Rose and Thistle and to Lila. Did he order her murder? And why did his name sound so familiar?

It wasn't only Lila's death anymore. I had Hanson's death on my hands. If the club was responsible for his death, the only way for them to do it was to have someone in the Dungeon do it. Either an inmate or a cop.

There was a note on the door to my apartment. It was from Mr. Ferguson telling me that he would try to have the work done on my place in a week. The apartment was bare, lonely, and breezy, at least in the bedroom.

It was before five. I had time to get on the horn to Dr. Burkholter. "Hey doc, I know where the blood came from that's on that rug I took you,"

"Hayden? What blood? What carpet sample?"

"The one I left in your office yesterday, from the Glisan place. Red on tan." There was a long pause. "I left it on your desk with a note."

"Hayden, I don't remember seeing anything like that. Say, I looked over that body you sent us this morning. What was his name . . . Carl Hanson?" It was my turn to pause. Was the old croaker playing it straight with me or was he jerking me around now? "Looked like suffocation to me, but I'm letting the kid handle it. He'll write a report in the morning."

"Suffocation? I didn't see any marks on his neck."

"Someone could have put a pillow over his face. But why am I telling you this? This is something you should have thought of."

"I'm testing you doc. So what about the pasting he got."

"That didn't kill him. The black eye was the worst of his injuries. You should have the report tomorrow."

"Davison's doing it?"

"Yes."

"Where did he go to school?"

"Some California school. Hayden, if there's nothing else, I've got to go. The wife and I have our weekly bridge game with the neighbors tonight."

"Yeah. I'll look for that report tomorrow. Hey doc, look for that rug tomorrow."

"Will do." The line went dead.

I set the handset back on the cradle, then picked it up again. When the desk sergeant at Central picked up, he told me that Sgt. Dekum had called in sick. I didn't think too much of it. What could he tell me that would make someone keep him from going in to work?

After showering and primping, it was time to go to Nora's. I made it only ten minutes late.

She met me at the door wearing a Navy sleeveless evening gown that accentuated her curves in the right ways. A slit ran up one stockinged leg to above the knee. She wore pearls on her neck and ears. She gave me the up and down with those emerald peepers of hers.

"If you are going to be late, it's good that you wore something that doesn't look like you bought it at the thrift store."

"For you baby, I break out the choicest glad rags I own. And what's wrong with thrift stores?" The suit I wore for the evening was a charcoal number. The only one I owned that I had tailored. This is the only suit I had that didn't scream cop.

She used the entire 20 minute drive to the restaurant telling me what had happened to her at school. I nodded, made the appropriate sounds and commented when I thought that's what she wanted. I had no idea the life of a schoolteacher was so dull. I was smart enough not to tell her that.

Not that I cared, hers was a voice that would make stock quotes sound sultry.

The Roadhouse was a joint outside of town. In ten years, the restaurant would be within the city limits.

The building was a gambrel-roofed affair. Brass hardware hung on the stained planking walls and doors. A quarter inch of varnish coated the ten-inch planks of the floor. This gave the wood a shiny glass like appearance. The furnishings looked like the sort you'd find at a five star joint. It had the look of a barn that took itself way too seriously. The same was true of the waiters.

After the waiter took our orders, Nora asked, "How was your day?"

"It was fine," I answered taking in the surroundings.

"You're not going to get off that easy. I want a real conversation. What happened to that Hanson guy?"

"Someone strangled him. I left orders for him to have been alone all night. Internal Affairs was all over me. I didn't touch the kid. When they found him he looked like someone roughed him up. When the autopsy report comes out tomorrow they will have to turn their sights elsewhere."

"So how did it happen?"

"Either one of the other cons did it or one of the officers did it. Either way there's a cover up." I leaned back in the chair, and stared at a point on the table.

"What's wrong, are you worried about Internal Affairs?"

"No, they're blind as a baseball umpire. Even they will have to accept the report. It bothers me though about Hanson. I didn't have enough to arrest him, I wanted to rattle his cage a little. If he wasn't involved with some dangerous people, he never would have met me."

She reached across the table, catching my hands in hers. My eyes traveled along her hands. Long dainty fingers lead to smooth thin hands and along to well shaped arms and finally to her face.

"Hayden, whatever happened to Hanson is not your fault."

"Of course it is. I put him in the Dungeon. That made him my responsibility."

"You can't control the actions of others." Her hands slid away from mine. "I don't understand you. Last night you killed two men outright you show no remorse about that. You made jokes. Now you're worried about one guy who died, who you didn't kill."

"Those two mooks last night knew what they were getting into. They were soldiers. They knew that they could end up getting killed. Hanson was a little toad who didn't know the rules. He didn't know, that what was in his head could get him killed."

"So you think there was some sort of conspiracy then?"

"There's nothing else it could be." A waiter came by, setting down her Merlot. "So those kids ran you ragged today?"

"No. I don't want to talk about them anymore. I saw your bookcases last night."

I smiled. "Yes."

"You didn't go to college. Those books are not the kind you'd see in a knuckle dragger's apartment, but that's what you show the world."

"I don't like the Carl Hansons of the world. They look down their noses at people and they don't have a single callus on their hand. They know the world from their ivory tower view and think they know the world."

"You don't fit with the knuckle draggers either."

"I pass."

"Why don't you use the GI Bill and go to college?"

"And do what?"

"Put some calluses in the ivory tower."

The waiter saved me by bringing our steaks. The conversation went other directions. I didn't want to think about college. I didn't want to think about the case anymore, but it was still there, in the back of my brain peeking out to taunt me.

After dinner and dessert, we went to a nearby county park to walk off steak and chocolate mousse. We found a bench where we watched the sunset. Then went to her place where we found another form of exercise.

CHAPTER 26

The Arizona

I was in the bowels of the ship. We were at port in Pearl. There was a whole lot of nothing going on. The other sailors and I were going about our duties.

An explosion rocked the ship. The deck jumped up and hit me.

Dungareed legs rush past to the nearest stairs. Hands help me up. I'm rushing to the stairs now also.

Another explosion. I'm slammed into a bulkhead. Ahead, I see the stairs. Thirty yards. Sailors in front of me, and behind. Everyone has a single goal in mind. Twenty yards. I hear tons of steel groaning under pressure. I hardly notice the ship is listing. Fifteen yards.

A wall of water explodes down the stairs. The water throws one sailor back against the bulkhead. His skull broke open. He falls dead on the stairs.

Lucky bastard.

We turn, running the other direction knowing we don't have enough time to make it to the next set of stairs.

The wall of water hits me in the back. I'm carried along like so much jetsam.

I hold my breath, swimming past pale bodies, through blood and oil, looking for a way out. I try to ignore the hollow distant sounds of the ship crushing under the weight of water. I try not to think of that same water crushing me.

Water creeps past the corners of my mouth down into my lungs. I want to panic, to thrash for the surface, before the battleship grey coffin closes in.

My eyes popped open. I'm covered in sweat. At first, I wasn't sure where I was. I looked around. There was a vanity against one wall. Next to it a free standing, full-length mirror in one corner. A warm body next to mine.

Nora's bedroom, I was in Nora's bedroom. Not the Arizona, not re-living my brother's death.

I eased out of the bed so as not to wake Nora. In my boxers and undershirt. I walked through the house to the front door and out.

Sitting on the front step, I looked up at the winking blanket of stars. I breathed in several long deep breaths. Trying to clear the images from my mind. Trying to clear the smells of salt water, oil and blood from my lungs.

That dream had been my companion since Dec. 7, 1941. That was the day the Japanese killed my baby brother, the day before I left the force and joined the Army.

It used to come four or five nights a week. I used to wake up scream-ing. In boot, they tried to section eight me. I wouldn't let them. I forced myself to stop screaming when I woke. I told them that the dream went away. I lied.

It visits less often now, only once or twice a week.

The sweat on my head, back and shoulders turned cold in the night air. I didn't mind.

I sat there looking at the stars listening to the night. In the distance, I heard the occasional car. Once, a cat stalked by in the yard across the street. I gobbled it all in trying to replace the dream world with the real one.

When the blankets on the bed did not seem so much like a death shroud, I made my way back to bed.

CHAPTER 27

Calluses

I woke to drumming rain. This was not the demure rapping of sprinkles. This was the insistent pounding of corpulent raindrops. Such is spring in the northwest. A bright sunny day followed by a soggy overcast one. Take that you damn robin. Hard to be singy and cheery in this weather, eh?

Nora was already out of bed. I could hear and smell cooking in the kitchen.

Once I showered and dressed, I joined her in the kitchen.

She stood facing the stove, away from me. I hugged her from behind, "Good morning." She turned in my arms choosing to say good morning in her own way.

While she finished with breakfast, I set the table. She had to direct me. I didn't remember where everything went.

Midway through breakfast, Nora asked, "What was wrong last night?"

"Nothing. Why?"

"You got up and sat out on the front steps. Are you sure nothing was wrong?" I looked away from her focusing on my plate pushing a piece of bacon around. "I wanted to talk to you then, but you didn't look like you wanted much company."

"It was nothing. I felt like some fresh air."

"That's why you thrashed in the bed before you got up?" Silence ruled as I stared at my plate and she at me. "OK, don't talk about it. I see what kind of relationship this is going to be." She resumed eating.

"I had a dream last night. It was about my brother. That's all. sorry I woke you."

"The one who was on the Arizona? You miss him? I'm sorry, that was a stupid question." We both resumed eating. Neither of us could ignore the heaviness lingering in the air.

"My old man was rarely home. Somehow, I got it in my fool head that my kid brother was my responsibility. When bullies beat on him on the play yard, I dished out my share of shiners along with a few busted noses."

"You haven't changed much." I looked up to see her smile. The smile lightened the mood.

"The time he needed me the most, I wasn't there. To make things worse, I couldn't have protected him anyway." She sat her fork down again. I looked up, wondering what she was thinking.

"That's what's troubling you about Hanson, guilt. You were responsible for him and you could not stop what happened. Hayden, you are not a god, not even a demigod. You are a man of flesh and blood, a hard man, but a man nonetheless.

"You can't control everything. The harder you try, the harder your life gets and the harder you get, until no one can penetrate that thick skin of yours." She reached across the table cupping my chin in her hand. "Not even me."

"You want me to change?" I asked, an edge in my voice.

"No. I want you to be aware that you can't do everything. Everyone has limits, I'm not sure you've found yours yet. Or worse, you haven't recognized them."

Both of us had finished breakfast. I sat back my forearms resting on the table. She sat forward, hands in her lap (a lady does not place her arms on the table I guess).

The silence was not uncomfortable. It was not pleasant either. I looked at my watch. "I'll help you clean up. I need to get going." Standing, I picked up my plate and silverware.

"Are you mad at me?" she asked, not moving.

"No doll, you're fine." We cleaned up the table and I helped her with the dishes.

"Marcus Aurelius said, 'If you are distressed by anything external, the pain is not due to the thing itself, but to your estimate of it; and this you have the power to revoke at any moment.' I must not be ready yet." I put a plate back in the cupboard, then turned and looked at her.

"Calluses in the ivory tower." She smiled and the last of the heaviness left.

At the door, she threw her arms around me. "Give me a call at noon?"

"Yeah, I'll call."

My walk to the car was dry as the rain had slowed. A glance at the sky told me this was a lull in the storm.

Nora had remained on the porch, waving as I drove off.

CHAPTER 28

Vincent Largo

If what Nora said was true, then that's why I had the tight knot in my gut. It could be why I felt denial. And it could be that she should mind her own damn business.

It could be that it was her business.

I left with no real idea about where I wanted to go. The funeral was not for a few more hours. My meeting with Fox was shortly before the funeral. I thought of going to the Kaufman house and harass Sally, but I thought better of it. The only thing to be gained by that was a headache. It'd be like talking to Chief Hewitt all over again. Only this time, half the size, twice the arrogance.

Most of the time that wouldn't bother me. Given my mood, I was liable to sock somebody if they started feeding me some song and dance routine. It wouldn't do to have that someone be a dame.

That led me to Vincent Largo. I didn't know him but I had the feeling that if I had to resort to pasting him, I wouldn't mind. The problem was, I didn't know where he lived.

Rather than go downtown, I dropped by an outstation.

After showing my tin, the desk sergeant allowed me behind the counter and directed me to a desk I could use. It was still early and the station was slow.

There were no Largos listed in the phone book. I tried the city directory.

There were several listings for Largo. Vincent was the only one I cared about. Vincent Largo had been living in the South Perry neighborhood for three years. He's unmarried and worked as a clerk in the DA's office.

Ten minutes, medium traffic, light rainfall and I was outside Largo's apartment building. I parked across the street from the parking lot. I didn't know which car was his, nor which apartment. I decided to wait.

Largo exited the building five minutes later. I was approaching his car as he opened the door. He was in his late twenties, my height, give or take, but I had twenty pounds on him. He was handsome and he knew it. He wore arrogance like a badge. His trench coat covered a suit that cost at least my month's salary. He held a black leather briefcase.

"Vincent Largo? I'd like to talk to you about the murder of Lila Glisan."

He turned, gave me the once over and said, "I don't know a Lila Glisan. Whatever this is about, it's going to have to wait. I'm very busy this morning." He had dismissed me and started climbing in his car.

"What for? Is there a young lady you need to disembowel or do you have a goat's head you have to plant somewhere?" He stood with his back to me and one foot was in the car. He stopped, seemed to think, then turned to face me.

"I don't know what you're talking about, but it is not at all humorous."

"Is that the first thing you learn in Pansy and Twig? How to lie?"

"If this is some sort of game you're playing, count me out." His eyes locked on mine. I'd face tougher challenges staring down a kitten. He turned back to his car. "Like I said, I have to leave."

"Tell me what it was like to listen to the tongue-less screams of Lila Glisan as you removed her guts."

"Come now, this is beyond the pale." He tossed the briefcase inside the car then walked back to face me. "Are you private or official? Whoever you are, I'm going to report you."

I flashed my badge. "Go ahead and fly your kite if you think it will do you any good. Look, since someone murdered Lila, hoods tried to do me in. My best suspect died. And I've heard stories about some strange group who has vague ideas about gaining power.

"I know you are in that group. I'm sure you had Lila Glisan killed. And I'm sure that somehow, the group had Carl Hanson killed. Do you want to make this easy for me and confess your sins now?"

"Are you going to arrest me?"

"Does this mean you're not going to confess?"

"Leave me alone until you have more than rumors to back up your allegations."

"You might as well suggest that the rain stop." The rain increased while he stood there wondering which card to play next. Soon it would be the big fat drops again. "Where were you three nights ago, the night she died?"

"Cormack McCollum's. He hosted a spring cotillion."

"Wrong, try again." He blinked and stepped back.

"Sally Kaufman and Nancy Mason can vouch for me."

"They'd be lying. Where were you?" He looked away. I grabbed his lapels pulling him to me so we were face to face. "Don't look away. I'm all that's important in your life right now. You've lied once already. Don't make it worse."

"I was here at my apartment. No one can vouch for me. I was alone. It's a poor alibi, but it's the only one I have. That's why I lied."

"Now we're getting somewhere." I let go. He took a couple of steps back. "Tell me about Rose and Thistle."

He hunched up his shoulders and held his coat tight against the rain. "It's starting to come down out here, could we go somewhere else?" I couldn't read him. I didn't know if he was cracking like Hanson or playing one over on me.

"I don't mind a little water. They murdered Lila because she was going to tell her father about Rose and Thistle. Who ordered the hit?"

I heard the crunch of gravel behind me. Largo looked over my shoulder.

That's when the lights went out.

CHAPTER 29

Spragg

I came to, sharp bits of gravel pressing into my face. I was face to face with macadam. The view was getting very boring. My head didn't want to move to change it. My eyes wobbled around in their sockets until a car tire came into view a few feet away. My head seemed to expand and contract with each beat of my heart. My stomach wanted to dump bacon and eggs on my new macadam friend.

Pushing myself up, I sat back on my ankles. Loose gravel cut into my knees. I hardly noticed through the fog that had engulfed my brain.

The rain had picked up while I was out and my clothes were completely soaked through. Turning my head up, I allowed the rain to splash on my face. That's when I noticed my hat was missing.

I felt the large knot that had developed on the back of my head where the sap bounced off my skull. Each time I touched it, a wave of nausea washed over my body. I gave up and sat there with my hands in my lap.

I could have sat that way forever for all my brain cared, but I couldn't allow myself to do that. "Must get moving," I thought. My body sat there with its own agenda. Instead, it decided to look around.

Largo's car was gone, but I found my hat. He must have run over it when he left. It looked like a foot wide pancake with tire tracks on it. At least I now had a goal.

I started to get up then stopped as the world swam around me. "Crawl over there you fool," I thought.

"No. Must stand up," I retorted. Great, they rapped me hard enough to break my mind in two. Now I was arguing with myself.

Through will alone, I finished standing and forced my guts to hold onto breakfast. On wobbly legs, I walked over to my hat. It was the longest ten feet of my life. Bending over to pick up the hat, I again argued with my stomach about who was going to do what.

I picked up my hat. After brushing off the dirt and grime and punching it back into shape I put it on my head, and stood there. My mind didn't want to focus on anything, except the little spots that swam in and out of view.

I looked down at my suit. It was a mess. Mud and bits of dirt clung to the lapels, shirt, and tie. The bastards had ruined one of my best suits. If I could get those little spots to leave me alone, I'd track down the bastards who did this and puke on their shoes.

Off in the distance, I saw my car. There was a seat or two in there. Hell, in the back was a bench seat. I could sleep on that for a while. Until say 1985.

My legs carried me to the car. Like a toddler figuring out what his legs were for, I stumbled at first, then more upright as I got to my car. The exercise seemed to have cleared my head somewhat.

Slumped behind the wheel, I wondered what to do next. Was Largo now my prime suspect? Or was he taken to keep him from saying anything to me? I had the nagging suspicion that one of us was under surveillance.

If he was, then my leads were close to drying up again. He'd be dead soon, if he weren't already. If I was the mark, then they were on to me. Not surprising, but how much did they know and who was in danger because they'd been with me?

I thought of Nora. If they wanted to get to me, they had their chance, why would they need her? That didn't put me at ease.

I started the car and drove to my apartment. I'm in the habit of checking for tails. Now I almost spent more time watching the road behind me than I did the road in front of me.

At my apartment I showered and changed into another suit. The shower helped clear away the cobwebs allowing me think about what to do next. On the way out I reached for the phone, thought better of it and left.

The writing on the glass in the door said DAVID SPRAGG and below that PRIVATE INVESTIGATOR. I opened the door, and a bell rang. I was in the waiting room of Spragg's office.

A second door opened. In the doorway stood a compact man. I had five, six inches on him, but he matched me pound for pound. His face looked like it had been on the receiving end of too many fists and pool cues. The thick calluses on flat knuckles said his thick meat hooks had made up for what had happened to his face. His suit had the color and appearance of a well used brown paper bag. The scowl he wore was enough to frighten a gorilla. At last, a kindred spirit.

"Hayden, what brings you by?" he asked around a smoldering stogie.

His voice had that rough quality that comes with too much smoking.

"I've got work for you." We had bumped heads on a few cases.

He'd never been a flattie, at least not around here and he was honest. He said what he thought and I'd never known him to cross the line. I couldn't say those things about any other shamus I knew.

"Come to do me a favor eh?" He chomped his cigar in thought. "Oh, hell, what is it?"

"A protection job."

His brows knit together. "Well, don't that beat all? A real cop asking a simple private op to do a protection job. What a sad state the department must be in. Better not let the newshawks know, there'll be panic in the streets."

"Are you done?"

"I could go on if you want. Come inside," he said pointing a thick thumb over his shoulder.

He took his seat behind an old desk that looked as rough as his face. I sat in an old and beat up wooden chair. The odor of stale cigar smoke held the room captive. The open windows allowing a fresh spring draft to glide through did little to clear the air.

"So who needs protectin'?" he asked putting his feet on the desk.

"A doll I'm seeing named Nora Hamilton. Some hoods I'm investigating might be willing to put a hurt on her."

"That doesn't explain why you came to me. You could get some bulls to do this. Is there something hinky with you two?"

"She's a school teacher." That's not much of an answer, but few school teachers are notorious criminals. He thought that over then plopped his feet on the floor.

"You think these hoods might have contacts in the department." I let silence be my answer. "Then I need to know more." I told him as much as I could about Rose and Thistle. The sapping this morning, Miss Kayer's encounter with a goat and Lila's murder. I glossed over the names. I didn't want to give too much information but I wanted him to know what he was getting into.

"I can see why you'd want someone watching over your dame. Sure, I'll do it." I told him where she was and what she looked like. Then we discussed fees and terms.

Any other shamus would have asked for a future favor instead of cash. Spragg didn't. He wanted things to be above board. That's why I went to see him.

CHAPTER 30

The Cemetery

I sat on a bench outside the cemetery. It looked like a peaceful park with hunks of granite here and there to break-up the monotonous green. A marvelous ten-foot wrought iron fence surrounded it. That was fine by me; I didn't want anybody in there getting out.

The funeral was to begin in half an hour. It was going to be one of those graveside numbers. They are fine when the weather is. Today, the weather was not fine. Neither was my mood. The rain was coming and going. It fell for a few minutes then eased off. We were between downpours.

I told Spragg not to let Nora know he was around. I didn't know for sure that there was a threat to her. I doubted there was but I didn't want to have another death on my conscience. I wondered what I feared more: her death or her death on my conscience.

A car drove up the opposite side of the street. It parked across from me. It was Fox. He sat in the car for a few moments, knowing what I had done and wondering why. When he built up the courage, he got out and crossed to my side. I checked both ways several times for traffic. I didn't want any more unfortunate accidents.

He wore a grey flannel overcoat and black patent leather shoes. He topped it off with a black fedora. The corners of his mouth were down and he walked in a stooped manner. He gave the impression of a man defeated or given up.

He sat down beside me on the bench. We stared in silence somewhere across the street. Besides my car parked down the street and his car, the street was empty.

"Why did you make me come here? If I had known where it was, I would have refused." His voice had the hollow quality that follows depression.

"Could be that I'm the kid who pulled the wings off flies," I replied, looking at him. My eyes traveled to the book he held in his lap. "Find anything?" He looked down to the book then his eyes traveled back across the street.

"I shouldn't be here. Can we go somewhere else?"

You spent the better part of a year sneaking around this bird. The only thing that stopped you from talking to her was fear. Now, the only thing stopping you is she's dead. Who knows, if you had talked to her, you could have spent that year with her instead of following her."

"She wouldn't have talked to me."

"Tell me Casanova, how do you know that? You don't. You don't know that until you try." His head tilted down until he was looking at the curb.

"What's in the book?" He handed it to me without looking at me.

"I marked the pages." Along the top of the yearbook, pieces of papers stuck out. I opened to the first page. It was a picture of the football team. He pointed to three guys whose necks could have doubled for tree trunks. Their names were at the bottom of the picture, along with the rest of the team. They didn't mean anything to me and I didn't recognize the mugs.

I turned to the next marked page. It was the same guys' senior photos. I thumbed through the other senior photos. Only Lila, Nancy and Sally looked familiar.

"Mind if I borrow this?"

"Fine by me." Fox stood and started for his car.

When he stepped off the curb, I said, "Fox." He turned, his shoulders and head slumped. "If you hadn't come forward, Lila's murder might've gone unsolved. It took a lot of courage to come forward." He stood a little straighter.

"Thanks detective. Let me know when you're finished with the book." The tone of his voice had gained some life, but not much.

He turned and continued to walk away. Before he turned, I noticed the corners of his mouth had turned up in a vague smile. He looked like a different man than when he arrived. He was less stooped and walked with purpose. I let him get to the middle of the street before calling him again.

"Fox." The vague smile still covered his face. "If I ever hear of you stalking a woman again, I'll beat the crap out of you."

His mouth turned down to a straight line and his shoulders sagged as if a ten-pound weight had dropped on them. Fox walked the rest of the way to his car, got in, and pulled away.

If he had waited another five minutes, he would have seen the funeral procession.

CHAPTER 31

The Funeral

I had gone to my car to wait for the funeral procession. According to the invite, there had been a brief ceremony at St. Michael's Cathedral. As brief as a Catholic ceremony can be. From there, the procession led here, Mt. Calvary Catholic Cemetery. I don't know who they were trying to fool. There were no mountains or hills.

Several blocks down a black car turned on the road driving slow. The vehicle announced its presence the way few other things could. It held a promise none could avoid and only a few welcomed. It's subtle threat all the more ominous because of its silence. Like a black cat stalking a mouse.

Four or five black limousines followed the hearse. Twice as many large black town cars followed. A pair of motorcycle cops (one from the city, the other from the county) escorted the group. Except for the cops, it looked like a mob convention was in town.

Behind all this was a collection of miscellaneous cars. These were cops, mourners, ass kissers and hangers on. I started my car. I drove in after them.

We took a winding route around mausoleums, statues, and simple headstones. We stopped somewhere in the back of the cemetery.

There was a large tent over the grave and chairs set up for the mourners. By the time I walked to the tent, the pallbearers were already carrying the coffin to the grave.

I stayed at the fringe of the crowd glomming over all the rich and powerful in attendance. Everyone from the governor to the dog catcher was here. There were also businessmen and newshawks buzzing around like flies over fresh roadkill. Les Carson was in the midst of everything. He bounced from one politician to the next asking for comments on Lila's death.

In the middle of it all was Senator Judge Glisan. He projected both strength and sorrow. The man carried himself with the sort of dignity that even the newshawks had to notice. He was a father in mourning, but he was also one of the most powerful men the state had ever seen. Glisan was not going to suffer fools. All who stepped near, beware.

There weren't enough seats for everyone. That was fine by me. I staked out a spot in the back in a corner so I could glom over the group. Bishop Doherty addressed the crowd. He spoke about Lila and her good works. He talked about the love of family.

I found myself thinking about my own eventual demise. That got me to thinking about the sap poison I received earlier. These pocket Napoleons had sent a chopper squad after me two nights ago. Why would they settle for a rap on the bean this morning?

It would have been easy enough to heft my carcass in the nearest car. Drive me to the woods and off me there.

That brought up the question of what happened to Largo. I had been operating on the assumption that one of his friends had beat on my noggin. If so, then why not kill me? This all suggested two things: there was a second group who didn't want to kill me, but did want Largo. Or Rose and Thistle had changed their mind about planting me.

None of this helped my headache. It actually made the headache spread to my hair.

Bishop Doherty led us through a few prayers. There was the obligatory head bowing, sniffling, and schnozzle blowing. When the prayers were through, Doherty signaled some workmen nearby. One of them pressed a button on the bier and the coffin settled into the grave.

Several women let out loud sorrowful wails, as if they had only now realized what was happening. As if there was a chance that Lila was playing an elaborate hoax on everyone. That she would jump out of the pine board and yell, "Surprise." If the screamers had only asked me, I could have shown them some pictures confirming Lila's death. It may not have made them feel any better, but they would have known for sure.

When Lila was in the grave, the workers moved the bier out of the way. The bishop scooped up some of the dirt from the grave with a trowel. He offered the trowel to Glisan. He stood, took it, tossed the dirt into the grave, then returned to his seat.

On either side of Glisan sat a man and a woman. I took them to be his surviving kids. The bishop refilled and offered the trowel two more times for each of the kids. When they finished, the bishop again signaled the workers who began filling in the grave.

One of the wailing women announced herself again. She still hoped Lila's fist would punch through the lid of the coffin as if this was a B movie.

People started filing past the Senator who remained seated in the front. He was hugging his other kids. Men placed a hand on his shoulder and mumbled a few words. Women stayed a bit longer in offering their condolences to him.

I had remained at my post observing the show at the front. Getting my fill of blubbering, I looked around. Some people were still seated and standing in the back. Motion caught my eye. Turning to the rear I noticed three men clustered together, talking. One had been looking at me. He looked away when I looked their way. I made no reaction. I turned so that I could watch the front of the tent, but keep the group in my peripheral vision.

They took turns looking at me then the rest of the crowd. They made a decision. One seemed to be leaving, but was moving to a space near my car. The others split up, moving to either side of the tent, attempting to blend in with the other mourners.

I made a decision too. It was time to talk to Glisan.

CHAPTER 32

Puppets

I went to the end of the line of mourners waiting to offer their condolences to Senator Judge Glisan.

"Hayden, thanks for coming. I missed you at St. Michael's," the barrel chested man said when I made it to him. He took my hand in both of his.

"I didn't make it there, I was making friends."

His red eyes searched mine for meaning, he gave up, and asked, "Have you met my other children? This is James Jr." Junior was a taller, thinner version of his dad and some ten years older than me. He offered his hand. "And my daughter Veronica Panas," Glisan continued. She was an elegant lady whose resemblance to her father was minimal. Along with her black dress, she wore a black hat with a black veil covering her eyes.

"Nice to meet you both. Did you have to travel far to get here or do you live in the area?"

"I live in Los Angles. I got in last night," said Junior.

"And I live in Seattle. I know why you ask detective. I'm eleven years older than Lila. We were never close. I didn't approve of her lifestyle. Any time I tried to offer advice, she resented it. Claimed I was mothering her. That's not to say I didn't love her, I did, but I was waiting for her to grow up."

"I knew her even less than Ronnie did. I left for college when Lila was only a few years old. But like Veronica, I did love my sister."

"Where did you two go to school?"

Both wondered why I would ask, but Veronica answered, "I went to the University of Seattle and my brother went to UCLA."

"Not Downing?"

"Father couldn't afford Downing when we went to school," she answered. I didn't detect any hostility or anger in Veronica toward her sister. She spoke in plain language. She was relaying facts.

The Senator asked, "Hayden are you any closer to finding Lila's killer?"

After excusing us to Junior and Veronica, I led Glisan to one side, away from prying ears, but not prying eyes. Several heads turned when I took the old man aside, including Les Carson and my boss, Chief Bowers. I stood so that I could watch the crowd and the three goons.

"Facta, non verba." I tested Glisan. I would have gotten more out of him if I said, "Silly Sally sells sea shells by the sea shore."

"What?"

"It's a hobby of mine. I collect stupid Latin phrases. You ever hear of Rose and Thistle? Did your daughter ever mention it?"

"I can't say that I have. What is this about Hayden? This Latin phrase? Asking Jim and Ronnie where they went to school? And what does it have to do with Lila?" Junior and Veronica were collecting a line of mourners waiting to speak with the old man.

"Judge—"

"Hayden, you are investigating the murder of my daughter, you call me James."

"OK. James, your daughter seems to have been mixed up with some twisted people."

"What do you mean? Was it drugs?"

"As far as I can tell, no." Relief spread across his face. "But she hooked up with a group at Downing bent on gaining power. What they plan to do with it once they have it, I don't know, but she was planning to leave the group and tell you all about it. I'm sure that's why they killed her. Did she ever mention a Vincent Largo?"

"Like my other children, I didn't know Lila as well as I should have, especially after she went off to college. I was a senator by then and I spend a lot of time back east. When her mother died, Lila and I . . . we had our difficulties. She needed me and I shut everybody out for a while." His reddened eyes looked away. "No, she never mentioned Vincent Largo to me. What kind of group is this, some sort of sorority?" The goons were getting impatient and nervous. One of the guys who came up to the tent walked back to the guy waiting by the cars.

"I wish it was. It's some secret society, like the Masons, only without the fun and laughs."

"Do you know who the leader is of Rose and Thistle? Is it this Vincent Largo?"

"No. They're very secretive. I'm sure Lila didn't even know who was in charge." Chief Bowers was sticking around for some reason. He was talking to people he wouldn't have given the time of day to.

"I visited with the mayor and wrote a letter to your chief asking the city to give you more help."

I must have been still addled. What James said didn't quite register. "What?"

"Hayden, in my time on the bench I got so I could read cops pretty well. When I laid eyes on you, I knew you were a maverick. But you need some help especially after what you told me."

"Thanks, but right now I don't need the help of anyone in the department. The night after Lila's murder a couple of gunsels tried to put me in here with your daughter. I wasn't sure who ordered the hit. I thought a guy named Hanson was involved. I threw him in O'Malleys." Glisan had been a judge long enough to know I was speaking about the lock-up.

"He took a beating and a dirt nap while he was in there. I didn't lay a hand on him. Now I've got some IA goons nosing around."

"What is this about?"

"I hate to say this, but I suspect someone in the department is with Rose and Thistle. They want to make this whole thing go away."

Glisan's face turned a shade of red that would make a lobster envious. He turned searching the crowd. Glisan started to signal the chief. I put my hand on his arm.

"Wait. I don't know who's involved." The anger clung to his face, refusing to let go. "I need to find that out before we rock the boat too much. You trust me to find your daughter's killer, now trust me in this." His face changed. There was still anger, but reason had crept in. "There is something you can do for me.

"See the gees over by the cars. I've seen the blond one a time or two at the downtown precinct. He's in IA. They're going to use Hanson as an excuse to question me, to see how much I know about Rose and Thistle."

"You think they're in Rose and Thistle?"

"No, they're corrupt. Rose and Thistle bought them. Or someone over their head is in the organization and gave them the order. Either way, they're puppets. I need you to get Bowers to get them off my butt.

A smile replaced the anger and reason on his face. "I can do that." He turned back to the crowd. "Bowers," he said sounding like an Army drill sergeant.

"Yes Senator?" Bowers asked when he made his way over to us.

"This is Detective Hayden. He is working Lila's homicide." Bowers looked at me with confusion on his face.

"Yes Senator, I know Detective Hayden."

"Is that so? Then why is your Internal Affairs harassing him? Is there some reason you don't want my daughter's murder solved?"

"I . . ." He looked at me again. "Well, a man he arrested died in custody. The autopsy report says the man suffered a beating. IA wants to ask a few questions."

"Hayden says the beating happened after he put him in O'Malley's. You should be talking to the boys down there."

"It's standard procedure."

"And if someone murdered your daughter, would you want that investigation impeded?"

"Well, no, but the department has standards—."

He looked at me again. I showed him my best poker face. Bowers sighed and looked back to Glisan. "No Senator Glisan, I would not."

"Then call off your dogs." Bowers seemed uncertain. "I know you intend to run for mayor some day. What you say next, could affect any endorsement from me."

Bowers sighed the sigh of a condemned man. "Yes Senator Glisan." He turned to me, daggers in his eyes, then stomped off to relieve the troops.

While Bowers was still in hearing range, I said, "Thanks James." Hearing me call Glisan by his first name, Bowers turned to catch the old man's reaction.

"You're welcome Hayden. If you need anything else, give me a call."

That was not the reaction Bowers expected.

CHAPTER 33

The Big Fish

On the way to the office, I kept checking my six, but I didn't pick up any tails.

At the office, I searched my desk for a copy of the autopsy report. I don't know why I bothered, I knew what was in it. Rather, I knew what should be in it. The chief had seen the report so where was my copy?

That's when I noticed how quiet the squad room was. There wasn't the usual chatting about cases, no phone calls, no typing, a lot of quiet. Looking around, most other detectives didn't meet my gaze.

It was time to go talk to Cap. I knocked on the door to his office. "Come in."

"What the hell's going on around here? Where's my copy of the autopsy report?" I asked after closing the door.

"The prodigal son has returned. Good morning, Hayden," said Cap.

"Oh, wait, I guess that depends on what your definition of good is. You might have had a good morning hob-nobbing with Senator Glisan. Some of us had to actually show up to work today."

"I was working."

"Oh, when did showing up the chief become part of your job description? Yeah, I heard about that. It might interest you to know that IA is serious about this investigation. And while you were at the funeral, I had three IA officers in here grilling me about you and your investigation."

"What's in the autopsy report?" Bartholomew sat back in his seat, a heavy sigh escaping his lips.

"It says you beat Hanson to death. That he suffered from massive internal injuries. That's why you don't have a copy of the report."

"That's bullshit. Burkholter said as much yesterday. Burkholter said he died of suffocation. And I didn't touch him. Whatever happened happened down there."

"Well, he didn't write the official report. Davison didn't submit it to Burkholter before he turned it in. I talked to Burkholter and he's going to submit another report, but the damage is done. IA has chosen to investigate, regardless what the Senator has to say about it."

"Andrews and Willis will back me up on this. They were there." Cap laced his fingers together, resting his head on them. "What now?"

"They have both sworn out formal complaints against you."

"What? This is a bunch of crap. It's time to cut the bullshit. Why was this dropped on me?"

Cap sat for a moment. I was beginning to think he wouldn't answer when he said, "I got a phone call the night she died. You know how it works. The call should have come from Sgt. Miller. It came from someone else. That someone told me to make it go away. I told them that was impossible. People would notice that Lila Glisan was dead. I told them that I had to assign this case to someone."

"What did I ever do to you Cap.? Why would you set me up like this?"

"Besides aging me, you've done nothing to me, but close cases. They wanted someone like George Ramsey. Someone who would play their game. But you're a son of a bitch, so I chose you."

"Thanks Cap. If I had known it was going to get mushy, I would have brought some flowers."

"Cut the sarcasm Hayden. You don't understand."

"Then make me wise."

"Admin hates you. They see the chip on your shoulder and that's all. Do you realize you are never going to rise any higher in the ranks than you are now? You might make detective sergeant when you get too old to cause any more trouble, but that's it.

"I know you don't give a crap about that, but I do. And when I get another promotion, I don't want it to be in a corrupt organization. So, when I got that late night call telling me to make this go away, I knew something was up. I had to choose someone who wouldn't play the game. Someone who doesn't even know the rules and wouldn't care if he did."

"So who called you?"

"I won't tell you that. You see, if I start ratting out my superiors, then this is the highest I'll ever go. If you find out who it is, you'll be a hero."

"Lot of good that'll do me. The rest of the department will hate me."

"The rank and file won't. This person is not well liked by them. Admin already dislikes you. Besides, you have protection that I don't." The wind dropped out of my sails. I finally got it. He played me like a marionette on a string.

"My buddy James," I said without enthusiasm.

"That's right."

"You didn't know that going in."

"You're right, I didn't. But I know the Senator. I was in his court lots of times. He's hard like you. But unlike you, he enjoys the game. I thought you two would hit it off despite that.

"Now get out of my office and figure out who did this." I had my hand on the door knob when he said, "Hayden, did you ever notice that picture of me by the door? The one where I'm standing next to the marlin?"

I'd noticed the picture before, but I'd not paid much attention to it. I looked at it again and I finally figured out how I knew Vincent Largo.

CHAPTER 34

Guido

Cap had been on the force a long time, long enough to know all the desk jockeys in the department. And, he loved to fish, as did many of the brass. Every summer he took a few weeks off to go fishing in California. He and the misses often went with other desk jockeys and their misses.

They'd charter a boat and spend their time fishing and drinking. I've often wondered about how those two seem to go hand in hand. Then I realized that fishing is so boring, you needed to drink to enjoy it.

The picture was from one of those trips. A smiling Captain Bartholomew was holding up a beer and standing next to a marlin hanging by its tail. Next to the marlin, also smiling, also holding up a beer was Charles Largo. That's Commander Largo to me.

The department has five precinct houses. A commander headed each. Central was Largo's bailiwick. He was in charge of, among other things, the Dungeon.

I didn't know Chucky well. I did know that he had served in the Marines. And I did know that officer plus military equaled college. Or was that college plus military equaled officer? You get the picture.

At my desk, I picked up the phone. When the operator came on the line, I asked her to connect me to Downing University. After a couple more connections, I managed to get to the records department. I found out that Charles Largo graduated from Downing. I also found out that he had a son, Vincent, who also graduated from Downing.

I pushed down the cradle, disconnecting the call, then made another, this time to the DA's office. They hadn't heard from Vincent. No, he hadn't called. Yes, that was unusual.

I hung up the phone, slouched in my chair and stared at the scratches on my desktop. I needed to find some way to connect Chuck to Lila and Hanson. I didn't know how to do that without tipping my hand. At this point, I didn't have a choice. About my only option was to rattle some trees and see what fell out.

I wanted to get out of the building before IA girded their collective loins again. I felt like I was in a den of thieves.

That aside, I needed to pay another visit to the Dungeon.

Dekum and the boys weren't all that happy to see me, I tried to hide my disappointment.

"What do you think you're doing down here," Dekum said coming to his feet faster than I would have expected.

"Paying a friendly visit Sarge. A guy likes to know who's setting him up. Tell me, which of you guys put the pillow over Hanson's head."

"Where do you get off? I'd thought you'd learned your lesson," chimed in the big guy who'd challenged me before.

"I guess I haven't had very good teachers sonny. You want to try to educate me?"

"You ain't half as tough as you think you are."

"Yeah, and you're twice as dumb as I think you are." There was much flaring of nostrils and the big guy puffed out his chest, but he didn't want to bite, not yet. "I don't have time to dance, but I'll keep you in mind if I need some light exercise." I turned away from Guido the wonder gorilla and spoke to the rest of the malcontents. "Look boys, a skirt is pushing up daisies, and for some reason, some cops are trying to get me to lay off it. Doesn't that seem hinky? Isn't it our job to solve crimes, not cover them up?"

"Our job is to play babysitter to a bunch of crooks. The job sucks. I'm not going to get out of it by bucking the guys upstairs," said Guido. One of his more lucid moments.

"Is it better being a lackey to a bunch of crooks? Come on sonny, don't be a palooka. You think those guys upstairs give a damn about you? They'll never move you up. You'll stay down here and rot in this place." It smelled like something already had. I didn't feel like telling them that.

The faces told the story. Some wouldn't look at me. Others looked at me out of the corners of their eyes. All said the same thing, "Get out."

"OK hotshot, you had your say and now you have your answer. Leave us alone," said Sarge.

I gave him the once over. His eyes were clearer than before.

"How's sobriety?"

"It's a bitch, but so is life."

"It's what you make of it." I looked over the assorted faces again. Seeing I wasn't going to get an answer, I went back through the gate and up the upstairs. I had reached the top when I heard someone come up after me. It was the big guy.

"What do you want sonny?"

"Wally Stehn. He works the night shift. He might tell you something." I thanked him, and he lumbered back down the stairs.

CHAPTER 35

Burkholter

I thought about checking with personnel for an address for Wally Stehn, but changed my mind. If I was being watched, I had to be careful about whom I talked to in the department. They would expect me to talk to the guys in the Dungeon. They wouldn't expect me to talk to Stehn.

I didn't need personnel anyway. Finding Stehn was eggs in the coffee. All I needed was the city directory, available wherever you buy fine books, and at my desk.

After finding Stehn's address, I paid Burkholter a visit. I caught him in the middle of a slice and dice.

"Hayden, good to see you," he said.

"And I'm dying to see you." The doc and I were the only people in the room, living that is.

"Sorry about the trouble with Davison. I don't know what's gotten into him. But we'll get it straightened out, you'll see." Burkholter had left his work and stood before me. He had the habit of gesturing with his hands when he spoke. Not something you want to be around when a guy has blood on his hands and a scalpel in his fist.

"Where is he?"

"I don't know," he said, raising his hands in the air. "I found a note saying he couldn't be in today, sick or something. He must have got in early, turned in the report and left the note."

"What's his story?" I asked nodding toward the table.

"Heart attack. Died last night at the hospital."

"No cops around then."

"No. I'm trying to get this business straightened out, but nobody wants to listen. I'm doing my best. I don't want you off the force, you're the only cop I can talk to."

"I'm the only one willing to over look that you're nuts." A peal of laughter that burst from his lips. I had to step back to avoid the bloody hand he tried to place on my shoulder. I have a one ruined suit per day policy. "Doc, this is important. You told me that Davison didn't go to Downing, right?"

He became serious. "I didn't tell you that. I said he went to school in California, medical school. He received his undergraduate degree at Downing. I thought you were asking about his medical qualifications. Why? What's wrong?"

"Do you happen to know where he lives?" He gave me the address.

I picked up a tail on my way to Davison's. It was a brown car, the driver kept it two lengths back and at least one car between us. I kept driving acting like I hadn't seen it. I didn't go to Davison's or Stehn's instead, I went to the South Hill.

You may not be able to read a book by its cover, but you sure as hell can judge a neighborhood by its appearance. First rule, the more rusting cars sitting in the front yard, the lower the income of the occupants. If there are lawns like putting greens, the occupants have nothing better to do than to slave over grass. Or pay someone to.

The easiest way to tell how ritzy an area, look at how straight the streets are. Straight streets equals no ritz. The more curves the more ritz. There wasn't a single straight street on the South Hill. My first three years on the force, the South Hill was part of my patrol area. I lost the car in the first minute.

Davison wasn't home. His house was on the edge of town. The city had built streets and put in the sewer, water and power lines, street lights and signs. There were few houses. Most of the lots were weeds and rocks. This annex would never make it—the streets were ruler-straight.

His was the only house on the block. All around were empty lots and fire hydrants to keep the weeds and rocks from burning down. The brown building was definitely a bachelor's house. The lawn was maintained, very little landscaping, and no flowers.

He had curtains drawn all the way around the house, including the back.

Most people didn't even know that this part of town existed. Hell, a leper museum would get more traffic than this place. So why the curtains?

I checked the front and back doors and the first story windows, all locked. The house had a basement with windows with wells dug away from the foundation. These windows also has curtains.

Now I was sitting in my car down the street, watching the house and feeling foolish. Ever try to stake out a lone house on an empty street?

I wanted in that house but I was too exposed. Night would be better.

CHAPTER 36

The Fight

I didn't find a pay phone until noon-thirty. It was in a drugstore. I closed the kiosk door behind me.

"I was beginning to think you didn't love me," Nora said after our hellos.

"No, I'm busy this morning, winning friends and influencing people. I'm not sure I can join you for dinner tonight."

"Does this have anything to do with this morning?"

"What? No, this has to do with a murder. You know that thing they tried to kill us over. I'm not mad now. I wasn't then.

"You weren't very happy this morning and you're late getting back to me." I sighed into the phone. It was a mistake I instantly regretted.

"What is that supposed to mean? Are you some sort of super man who doesn't need anyone? Do you think pain is only for the weak? I saw you in pain last night and I wanted to help and you got mad at me."

"I don't like talking about my brother, that's all. It makes me uncomfortable. What you said this morning hit a little too close to home. But none of that has anything to do with not going to dinner with you tonight. It has everything to do with a murdered young lady. Murdered by someone who has ties to the department, the DA's office and who knows what else. Don't play Freud on me."

Stony silence was my reward. A man came in the drugstore, looked around, saw me and drifted to a magazine rack as though waiting for me to finish.

"Nora?"

"I don't want to talk to you right now."

"Fine."

"What do you mean, 'fine'? If this is going to work, we have to be able to talk and you're not making it easy. What is it about you men, especially you? You spend all day talking to people, it's your damn job." She had my attention now. "And you still don't know how to talk to me." What could I say? I sure as hell didn't know.

"Hayden, I don't know how, but despite your gruffness, I'm falling in love with you. I don't get that feeling from you."

"If that were so, would I hire a private op to protect you." That was met with uncertain silence. The guy waiting for the phone gave up and left.

"What?" I explained to her about my meeting with Largo and about Spragg.

"What was I thinking? I had an idea that dating a police officer would leave me fearing for him at times. But how was I to know that my life would be in danger also?"

"Your life is not in danger."

"Then why do I need a body guard?"

"It's a precaution. I don't know what to expect from these goons, I wanted to make sure you were safe."

"Because you love me or because you don't want another death on your conscience?"

"That's low." I let the words sit there, like an eight hundred-pound gorilla.

After a moment, I said, "Promise me, you'll listen to Spragg. I trust him, and you should too."

"Fine. How is your apartment coming along?"

"It's not done yet."

"Are you coming over tonight? You need some place to sleep."

"Sure, thanks. I should let you go, your kids are waiting." We said our good-byes. I put the handset back on its cradle. The coin jangled down through the phone into the bank. I wondered what had happened to my boring ordinary life.

CHAPTER 37

The Tail

When I pulled away from the curb, I noticed a blue Packard pull out at the same time. The Packard followed for about ten blocks, then turned off. I turned on to a busier street. I saw a familiar brown car, but then it turned off. In the next block, I noticed the blue Packard turn on the street several cars back.

I switched through the bands on the police radio. It took some work, but I finally found what I was looking for. The riders in the Packard were coordinating the tail. It sounded like two cars. On cue, the Packard turned off. In the next block the brown car pulled out one car back. They were doing a good job, most people would not have noticed the tail at all. I had an advantage over most people. I had recently become paranoid.

At the next traffic signal I set the brake on the car, drew the 1911 and got out. Hiding the gun behind my leg I walked back to the brown car ignoring the irate driver in the car behind mine.

The driver of the brown car tried to ignore me as I approached. The passenger stared in disbelief. I had seen the driver before reading mags at the drugstore. I didn't recognize the passenger. They must have brought them in from other precincts.

The driver of the car behind mine started honking the horn. The signal must have changed. Standing in front of and to one side of the brown car, I brought my gun around and fired three rounds into the radiator. It let out a loud hissing sigh and dumped water on the ground.

Smiling, I tipped my hat to the bulls in the car and walked back to mine.

Any other time I would have handled that a different way. I was not in the mood and did not have the time to play nice. I also wanted to send them a message: mess with me and I'll mess with you.

That left only one tail to shake. By now the lugs in the brown car had buzzed the Packard. Whether they'd keep it up, I didn't know, but I wasn't going to give them much time to think about it.

With the gunshots, the honker gave up. If he hadn't parked so close behind me, he might have been able to leave the scene. Instead he was sitting behind the wheel trying to blend into the seat.

The signal changed when I was in the intersection. In the mirror I saw gawking witnesses. They swiveled their heads between the brown car and me like King George VI at Wimbledon. I was not concerned about them, I was keeping my eye out for the Packard.

At the next street, I turned off and took the next alley. I dodged garbage cans and cats looking for scraps. Barreling through I crossed the streets without looking. After several blocks, I turned back on to the street. I was in a residential area.

I slowed down again. I didn't see the Packard anywhere. It would be harder for the car to tail me now because there were fewer cars to hide behind. I stayed on the side streets all the rest of the way to Stehn's apartment.

He lived in Browne's Addition. It used to be home to the upper crust. Then they realized that the streets were windier on the South Hill and began the migration there. As the rich moved out, their large homes became apartment houses.

Stehn's was a three-story brick affair that at one time had been a modest five bedroom, four fireplace home. The building's new owners shoehorned two apartments in on each of the first and second floors. They turned the small third floor into an apartment of its own. According to the mailboxes by the front door, Stehn lived on the top floor. Didn't anybody live on the first floor anymore?

I went down a hallway on the main floor that split those two apartments.

At the back I found the stairs. On the second floor was a landing with two doors. The stairs doubled back on themselves, ending at a door. The hinge-side of the door had a corner cut out to accommodate the low roof. I listened at the door. I didn't hear anything. That didn't mean much. If he worked the night shift, he still might be sleeping.

I tried the knob. It didn't turn. A little work with my picks and the door opened a couple of inches.

It was a studio. The door opened on a corner. A small wedge of light showed from the open door through the darkness. A kitchenette was to the right of the door. A small table and four chairs sat near the "L" of the kitchenette.

Beyond the table, in the wall I saw two more doors. These doors were six inches shorter than usual, again, to accommodate the roof.

I opened the door a little more. A large window in the front wall was the only window in the main room. A blanket covered the window, explaining why the room was so dark.

I stepped into the room, closed the door with the knob still turned and released it so it made no sound. I remained where I was, allowing my eyes to adjust to the darkness and listening for any sound. I heard nothing except light breathing punctuated by the occasional snore.

The rest of the room emerged from the darkness. The kitchenette was still to my right. I could now see what the door had blocked before.

Straight-ahead was a couch. Beyond that were a bed and a sleeping form. The ceiling followed the pitch of the roof. The highest point of the ceiling ran from the window to one end of the kitchenette.

I walked to the doors on the other side of the room. The closest one to the kitchenette was the bathroom. Nobody hiding in there. The next was the closet, also free of thugs and other things that go bump in the night.

I pulled back the blanket over the window, peeking out. Everything looked Jake. There was no blue Packard. No one standing around trying to look inconspicuous.

Beside the bed, under the window was a small table with a drawer, a lamp, and a phone on top. Judging by the snoring, Stehn was fast asleep, I took a chance and opened the drawer. Nestled under some skin magazines was a .38 revolver which fit in my coat pocket.

I grabbed a chair from the dinner table and set it by the bed. I took a seat and turned on the lamp. Stehn groaned and rolled over, taking the sheets with him. The snoring resumed. I try to be a nice guy and wake him and what does it get me? Squat.

I reached my foot out and kicked the bed. The other side was against the wall, so my end of the bed jumped up in the air.

"What the hell?" he asked sitting up, braining himself on the pitch of the roof. That's when he noticed me. He dove to the table, yanking the drawer out. His hand dug under the mags.

"Those aren't going to do anything for me, I got the real thing at home." He sat up against the headboard of the bed and pushed back in the corner as much as the roof would allow. His eyes showed whites all around his iris. I reverted to my bad cop role. I showed him my scowl that had sent more than a few Guidos packing.

"Look, I did what you guys wanted. I didn't rat you out. I'll stay quiet you don't have to worry about me. That guy Hayden doesn't know a thing. IA's after 'im. He's under glass right now. I'm no squeal. Don't hurt me. I'll do anything you want."

I let his verbal diarrhea run a little longer. He didn't say anything worthwhile, he was bumping gums. He finally stopped and sat there with his head craned against the wall. He was breathing and sweating like he'd run a marathon.

I reached in my coat and he let out a loud piercing squeal. He scrunched his eyes closed and held up his hands to ward off the bullets he was sure was on the way. I removed my shield and opened the case so he could see the badge. Little good it did, his eyes were still closed. When he didn't hear the explosions, he opened his eyes.

They focused on the badge. He relaxed and his breathing slowed. "You had me worried. So do you guys have him yet?" I turned the case around so he could see the ticket. He moved closer, squinting, his lips moved as he read my name. "Oh, shit." He pushed himself back into the corner, looking even more terrified than before. "Don't kill me. Don't kill me," his voice was a whine.

"Why would I do that?"

"Because I set you up. I'm sorry, they promised me a ride out of the Dungeon. I had to do it. I can't take it there anymore. I need to get out of there."

"You smoke?" He looked at me, unsure if I was on the level.

"Yeah. You got a smoke? I could sure use one right now." I returned the badge, letting him see the 1911 as I opened my coat. He flinched again. I dug in the other side of my coat for the pack of cigarettes. I held them out. He watched the pack, then me. One shaking hand reached for them. When his hand was inches away, I pulled the cigs back.

"You haven't earned them yet. Not until you sing." His eyes studied me. "I already know about Largo."

"When you were on your way to the station, he called me and the sergeant up to his office. He knew Hanson was coming in. Andrews and Willis called ahead on the radio. They're in his pocket. Money from various rackets, some collecting and enforcing for his friends.

"He called us up and told us that Hanson shouldn't make it through the night. That's how he said it, 'shouldn't make it through the night.' He told us how he wanted it done and that he'd take care of the cover up."

"Who did it, you or the sergeant?"

"He did, I played lookout while he put the hurt on Hanson for a while. They wanted to make it like you busted him up. When he had enough, the sergeant knocked him out. Then he put the pillow over Hanson and smothered him."

"What about the other guys on the shift?"

"Far as I know, they're clean. Commander Largo called them all up to his office. Gave them some sort of pep-talk or something."

"How does the Chief figure in?"

"I don't know. I don't know anything about the chief." I watched him for a few moments. Everything he said fit. I figured most of it, I needed a witness to tell me for sure.

I'd noticed earlier that the bathroom door had a lock on it. I got up, crossing over to the bathroom. I took his gun out of my pocket, emptied the rounds into my hand. I took a towel and wiped the gun and tossed it on the floor. Then I locked the door and took the key. I wiped the bullets and put them in the closet under some blankets, he would have to search for them.

I didn't know the history of the piece. Who knows what it had been used for or would be used for if my prints were on it.

I moved back to the bed, grabbed the phone from the table and ripped the cord out of the wall. "You'll understand if I don't want you making calls for a while." I sat back down and tossed him the pack of cigarettes. He grabbed them out of the air like he was a shortstop for the Giants.

"This business is almost over. When it's done and you've testified, and you will testify, you will quit the force, if you're not booted off or in prison. That's not a suggestion. I don't want anyone I don't trust checking my six.

"This is a suggestion: move out of town when this is over. I won't hassle you unless you're doing something illegal. There are going to be some loose ends to this case that I can't tie up. There are too many interested third parties. And they might want to wipe the slate clean."

I got up and started for the door. Standing on the stairs, I held up the bathroom key. "This will be in your mailbox."

CHAPTER 38

The Stash

Largo had Hanson chilled off. I could think of several reasons. One, Rose and Thistle was afraid he'd tell me too much. Or two, they wanted to set me up. Three, they wanted to kill two birds with one stone.

If they killed him because he might tell me about Rose and Thistle, then they thought he was the weak link. They had the most to lose if he talked. What could he tell me that Sally and Nancy could not?

From what I knew, he was higher on the food chain in the organization.

He would know more names and more of the organization's activities.

There was another possibility. What if they wanted Hanson's death to scare me off. All that did was make me mad. I'd had no problem showing it. That's when they thought about setting me up.

None of that let me shake the feeling that Hanson died for a bigger reason. That's why I was sitting in my car a block away from his apartment building. I was watching every car like it was a Panzer. Listening to the police radio like I was scanning German radio frequencies.

After sitting there for half an hour, I hadn't seen any suspicious traffic or people. I got out and walked up and around several blocks. I didn't spot a tail.

Were they getting better or were they not here?

Certain I was in the clear, I went in the building. I used the fire escape and an open second story window. Just because you're paranoid, doesn't mean you don't have enemies.

His apartment was like I'd left it. That is to say, it still had four walls and a door. It looked like someone, several someones, had been in to do some rearranging.

My place had bullet holes in the walls. I was in no position to judge another's interior design. But whoever had done this subscribed to a place for everything and everything in its place. So long as that place happened to be the floor.

Someone had moved the piano from the wall exposing its open back. Broken furniture and sliced upholstery littered the floor. The bedroom was much the same, except here someone dumped out dresser drawers. The whole apartment was like this. They had tipped over every piece of furniture. Everything on top of the furniture was on the floor. I navigated around books, clothing, kitchen utensils, pencils and paper. A camera (no film), family photos and all the rest of Hanson's worldly possessions were also on the floor.

I felt like giving up and finding some other tree to bark up, but I couldn't. I still had a job to do. Lila mixed with some crazy people, but she didn't deserve what she got.

If I were going to find anything, I would have to think like Hanson. I gave that up because it hurt too much. I couldn't think like a slimy little weasel.

But he was a clever slimy little weasel. That someone smashed up his rooms showed he had something to hide. He would have to know that someone would come looking for it.

He was clever but I doubt he was good with his hands, they were too soft. That ruled out hiding things in secret panels or false bottoms in drawers. Hanson wasn't the type to use tools. He wouldn't know a handsaw from a hacksaw. So why was there a screwdriver lying on the kitchen floor?

Tools in kitchens aren't uncommon in most people's junk drawers. I didn't see any other tools, not even a hammer and nails. The guys who did this must have taken the screwdriver for granted. I didn't have the luxury.

I took the screwdriver through the apartment, looking for things to use it on. I took heater vents off the floors and walls. Switch plates and outlet plates were next. I took apart his phone. I even took apart the ceiling fan in the bathroom. That's how I found myself in the bathroom, staring at the mirror. It was a nice mirror. It wasn't a medicine cabinet. It was an honest to goodness mirror. Attached to the wall with little plastic clips.

My reflection stared back at me as I thought about it. What could be between the mirror and wall? In the end, it was simple. What the hell else did I have to lose?

After unscrewing the fasteners, I set the mirror on the floor. I already had enough bad luck, I didn't need any more.

Hanson wouldn't have known how to use a saw, but he knew how to use a camera.

Tacked to the wall were six 8x10 glossies. Each taken at a distance, some were blurry and grainy. Together they told the story of a romance. Not a romance so much as sex.

The dame was pretty, she looked good in the buff and she was young. It sounds nice. It sounds like the sort of thing most guys would do. It's not something a married man should do. It's not something the married chief of police should do. Especially when that young dame is a socialite named Sally Kaufman.

CHAPTER 39

A Thousand Words

I stared at the photos, in disbelief. I felt the way a child would seeing Santa Claus in his house on Christmas Eve.

I took down the pics, still not quite believing what I had. Behind one of them was an envelope. Inside were the negatives of these and several other photos. This was Christmas.

I got out of there after putting the mirror back. I left the building the same way I went in and took the scenic route back to my car.

I found a five and dime. I bought two manila envelopes and a letter envelope. In one of the manila envelopes, I put four of the photos. I sealed it and jotted a note on the outside before stuffing it into the other one. I jotted a note on the envelope with the negatives and dropped that in the letter envelope.

I found a post office and mailed each to a different address.

The pics were revealing and I don't mean Sally and Bowers. I recognized the room they were in. Hanson took the photos on different days. The clothes Sally and the chief wore, when they wore any, were different. One thing that remained the same was the location. I had been there. It was the spare bedroom in Lila's house.

That left a bad taste in my mouth. How much had Lila done for Rose and Thistle before she wanted to quit? What was she involved in?

What bothered me more was the chief. I hardly knew him. I'd only said five words to him in the past year. I hardly thought he would do something like this.

The time was well past lunch, approaching dinner. My stomach was telling me that if I wanted its cooperation for the rest of the day, I needed to find something to eat. I surrendered and drove to Frank's. I figured it had to be safe because I was the only cop who ever went there.

"You don't look so good Hayden, like a ghost was after you," Frank said when I set the bell off over the door.

"The only ghost after me is the last meal I had here." Frank took my order at the bar, a Ruben, and I went to use the pay phone in the corner.

"Glisan residence," came the butler's stiff voice, after two rings.

"Yeah, this is Detective Hayden."

"Hello detective, if you will please hold, I will get Master Glisan for you."

"Wait, you're the one I want to talk to."

"Oh?" He sounded like I'd asked him to run naked across the stage of Carmen while the president sat in the balcony.

"I need to ask you some questions about Lila."

"I ought to refer you to Master Glisan."

"Do I tell you how to polish the silver? Then don't tell me how to do my job. Who lived with Lila at her house in town?"

"I would not know what you are talking about sir."

"So James doesn't know, does he?" The silence told me all I needed to know. "Look, someone played Lila for a fool. People thought they could gain some sort of influence through her. When she finally figured it out, she tried to bail on them, but they wouldn't let her."

"Then why do you need to ask about who may have lived in the house?"

Frank caught my eye as he sat the Ruben in my usual spot.

"I need confirmation. Tell me if this is the way it played out: Sally lived there too, at least part of the time. And sometimes Lila stayed up there in Shangri-La, while Sally used the place in town for her own purposes."

"I can't speak to the motives, but yes, you appear to have figured out the arrangement."

"Yeah, like a blind man stumbling in the dark. Thank you for your help."

"Sir, should I inform Master Glisan?"

"Should he find out from a trusted employee or a police officer?"

"Does he need to know at all?"

"It's going to come out no matter what I do."

"I understand sir. Have a good day." I said as much to him, then went to eat my sandwich.

CHAPTER 40

The Brute

While I was eating, I figured out what to do next. Food helps me think. Finished, I went to the phone and called the Kaufman's.

"Hello?" asked a pleasant sounding woman.

"Sally?"

"No, I am her mother." No butler and no maid to answer the phone? I was being jipped.

"I would have guessed sister. Is Sally home?"

"I'm sorry, I didn't catch your name."

"Detective Hayden. I'm investigating Lila Glisan's murder. Is she home?"

"She's not here." The voice had become icy. "She's not going to be available for a while. You could have spoken to her at the funeral you know."

"If she'd been there, I would have."

After a pause I could have boiled an egg in, she said, "She wasn't at the funeral? You must be mistaken. There were a lot of people there I'm sure."

"The weather was bad enough to drive off all but the most devout sycophants. That left about a hundred able to attend. And lady, I've seen enough of your daughter lately to recognize her. She wasn't there."

Another pause. "Is she in some sort of trouble?"

"Does blackmail qualify? Look, I don't know how much trouble she's in and I can't figure out for sure by playing twenty questions with you. I need to find her."

"She's at the train station. She's going to visit her grandmother in Salem. She said she needs to get away for a while." Yeah, she needed to get away. I asked what time the train left. She told me. I thanked her and hung up.

The train station was dying. It wasn't the station's fault. People were falling in love with airplanes. It was sad in a way. The station was a grand palace made of brick and marble. It had columns supporting a ceiling tall enough for geese to migrate through.

The city designed it to make you feel like you were going on a fantastic journey. Even if all you were doing was going to visit relatives. After visiting with them for five minutes, you remembered why you moved in the first place.

I found the track for the Salem train. She wasn't waiting there. I checked the other tracks. I found her at the Seattle track.

I stood back in the crowd watching for anyone who might be with her or watching her also. From outside, I heard the unmistakable growling of an engine. People began pressing forward to the platform. She remained alone and she looked like she expected to.

I moved to the edge of the crowd to within fifteen feet of her. She didn't see me. She was too busy looking down the track. The train crawled into the station like an arthritic dinosaur. The crowd moved to where they thought the doors would stop. It looked like Sally would be some distance from one.

The train finally stopped, sighing relief from its brakes when it did. The crowd plodded to the doors. I kept a few paces from Sally. She wasn't good at navigating the crowd and began to fall back. When she was feet from the door, I was the only person behind her.

I grabbed her arm. "Miss, I need to speak with you." She looked over her shoulder to put up some kind of protest. She saw me and panic flashed in her eyes. I had my tin out for all to see, including someone who would come to the aid of a maiden. "Can we go over here to talk?" I asked pointing with the tin, giving even more people a chance to view my pretty ornament. I didn't give her a chance to answer. Holding her arm I towed her to the side.

"Your grandmother move without giving notice to her daughter?" I asked when we were far enough away from prying eyes and ears. "That daughter thought her own daughter had gone to her best friend's funeral this morning. Everyone is a bit confused."

"Well detective, something came up and I had to spend the morning packing. You'll have to excuse mother, she's a bit distressed. You see, I'm going to visit my grandmother, my fraternal grandmother. She's having some heart problems."

"That's good, because I didn't know which grandmother you were visiting, I guessed."

"I'm sorry about the confusion. Now if you will excuse me, I have a train to catch." She started to turn away.

"I'm not done with you yet," I said grabbing her and turning her back around. "Whose idea was the house? Hers? Yours? Rose and This-tle's?"

"I haven't a clue what you're talking about."

"Was it Hanson? Was it some job you were doing for your little social club? But that doesn't add up. I thought Rose and Thistle was after power, not some high-class prostitute ring." Her hand lashed out to slap me, I caught her hand before it reached my face.

"You brute. How dare you suggest any such thing?"

A Good Samaritan was taking in the conversation. He started walking toward us. I flashed him the badge, "Go find an old lady to help cross the street, Jasper." Back to Sally, I said, "You're right. I am a brute. Civilized people have another word for prostitution, but I don't. Before you get too handy again, you should look at this." I slipped the photos out of my coat. One showed them kissing, while clothed. The other showed Sally and the chief kissing, not clothed.

"So why did you do it? Why would you turn on your friend? Was it because her father was richer than yours? Or was it because he could give her everything that yours couldn't give you? Did Lila know why you wanted to use her house? Did you even care about her or did you look at her as a cash cow?"

Her face scrunched up and turned red. "Very convincing. Now can you bring on the tears?" She let out a loud wail and the waterworks began. "Nice, I'm sure it works well on your father." She reached for her purse, I grabbed it from her before she could get her hand inside. "Not so fast."

All she had in it was money, a driver's license, makeup and some tissues.

I gave her the tissues. I thought she needed a reward for such a convincing show.

"Can it will you? Save it for a drought." She was right, I was a brute. The tears looked genuine. I felt like a heel for making her cry but I couldn't stop. I didn't want to stop. For reasons I couldn't put my finger on, I wanted her to realize what she had done. I wanted for her to feel remorse.

"The chief is a moron. How do you think he became chief? Sure, he didn't have to take you up on your offer. But then again, you didn't have to make the offer did you?" She blew her nose into one of the tissues. "How do you think his wife will feel when she finds out? What did she do to you that you had to stick your nose in her business?"

"You don't understand." She was mopping her face without much effect; the tears kept pouring down. Her makeup was a mess.

"I've made that clear."

"I was finally part of something, something bigger than myself. We were working together toward a common goal. They needed a way to the chief and I volunteered. But I didn't have anything to do with Lila's death. I knew she wanted out, but I didn't know they would kill her." The tears were slowing.

"Yet you stood by."

"I didn't want to be next. I still thought I could be part of it. Until they killed Carl."

"Is he the one who took the pictures?"

"Yes. He hid in the closet while we . . . Lila didn't know about it. She thought it was Carl and I, she had no idea there was anything else to it."

"Did they threaten you?"

"No. I wanted to get away until this had blown over."

"What happened this morning that you didn't go to the funeral?"

"I wanted to go. I was driving there, but I knew Senator Glisan would be there and I couldn't face him. I drove around until I thought I had been gone long enough, then I went home. I wasn't sure what to do when I got there. After a while I got the idea to leave."

She patted her face with a sodden tissue held in a shaking hand. The conductor yelled, "All aboard." Her eyes pleaded with me. "You've committed a crime. I can't let you go."

"What about my bags? "

"Guess you'll have to make a trip to Seattle in three to five to get them back. Come along."

Second Chances

She was a quiet little mouse all the way to the jail. The sheriff's cooler was near the courthouse, not far from the train station.

My world used to be like the westerns, except the good guys wore shiny pieces of metal instead of white hats. Now someone had played a trick on me and gave some of the bad guys badges. I didn't know the good guys from the bad. And the bad guys killed the last person I had locked up. Granted, that was the Dungeon, our corrupt little hole. Did I know this place was any better? If it wasn't, one of the deputies inside might tip off Rose and Thistle about my whereabouts. And they might kill Sally too. That might bring too much attention to them or it might be another chance for them to set me up.

I sat a block away from the jail considering my options. She sat in back without the hint of an expression on her face.

She seemed to have resigned herself to whatever I decided to do.

"Give me your purse." She handed it over the seat, no questions. I dug out her driver's license, tossed the purse back. Watching her in the mirror, I asked, "How do you feel about playing one of the great unwashed?"

"What?"

"If I take you to the jail, everything should be Jake. But I don't know that for sure. Also, I don't want any other cops to see me right now. I could take you to the poor farm as a Jane Doe vagrant. You'll be safe there. I don't know why Rose and Thistle would have contacts in such a place. As long as you don't call anyone, nobody will find you."

I put my arm over the seat and turned to face her. "When this is all cleared up, I can get you out and we'll go from there. That Jake with you?"

"What do I have to do?" She leaned forward a little in her seat. She was worried about the jail too.

"It's a farm. There's corn, potatoes, carrots, they even have some livestock. You'll have to work in the fields, but at least you'd be outside. You can't leave the farm, but you'll be with other people, working toward a common goal."

A faint smile turned up the corners of her mouth. "I can do that." I faced the front and drove out to the west side of the county to the poor farm.

CHAPTER 42

Trophies

The people at the poor farm didn't want Sally. Her performance won them over. Hell, I felt like giving her some loose silver.

She told them she was from back east, a small farming town in Indiana.

Her father had abandoned his family when he got back from the war. He left Sally and her mother and her four younger brothers and sisters to fend for themselves.

Now, her mother was in a hospital back east, dying from cancer. She had come here to find her dad. She was hoping that he could find it in his heart to help the woman he had once loved. My part was to tell them that I caught her stealing some fruit and it was better for her to be at the poor farm than jail.

The clincher came when she let loose the tears. She was describing how she and her siblings had to pull the plow. It seems that the mule had died and her mother couldn't afford to buy another.

It sounds stupid, but her wailing tears almost brought the bleeding hearts to tears too. I didn't know whether to laugh or punch them.

I took my time driving to Davison's. I had nothing else to do. I wanted to check on Nora, but the less time I spent around her right now, the better. I still checked for tails. I still didn't see any. Had my warning been enough? I couldn't quite convince myself of that.

When I drove past Davison's, the place was quiet. No cars, and the curtains were still keeping out the world.

There was still about two hours until night fell. I used the time to scout the area. To find out where the roads around the house led. Which were dead ends and which were outlets.

Davison's was not the only house in the new development. I noted where those were and how to get there. I found several outlets that might be useful. The street by Davison's seemed to be the main street in the development.

When I finished, I parked several blocks away. From my vantage, I could see Davison's and two other houses on different blocks. Anyone, who saw me, wouldn't know which house I belonged to.

As darkness wrapped her cold arms around the city, I dug a flash out of my glove box and started for the house. The city had put in street-lights. The coyotes and other creatures of the night used them. They had not learned that this was no longer their territory.

I opted for cutting through the empty lots. There was still enough light that I didn't need the help of the arc lights nor my flash.

The house was still locked. There were two locks on the front door. The lock in the knob and a deadbolt. On the back there were three. The garage door was also locked. The windows had no locks, other than the cheap latches.

A chain is only as strong as its weakest link and that was never so true as it is with windows. It was a simple matter to slide my knife between the sashes and push the latch back and I was in.

The sun had set. That didn't stop it from being midnight inside. I turned the flash on. My surroundings took on a dull red glow. I was us-ing a red lens. It's less noticeable from the outside.

I played the red beam across a very plain, clean kitchen. A rack by the sink held dishes set there to dry. There was nothing interesting in the kitchen. Unless you find canned goods and pots and pans interesting. I checked the fridge. No goat head. I guess he was safe for now.

The first and second floors were as boring the kitchen. I did as good a search as I could without tossing the joint. Everything was neat and tidy. Nothing lying around.

The couch and chairs in the front room were not new, but in good condition. The dining room table carried the shine of deep polish.

The floor of the garage was missing the usual oil stain. The bathtubs upstairs and down didn't have a ring around them and the toilet seats were down.

Davison had made the beds in the guest room and the master bedroom upstairs. He creased the corners. I thought I was in boot camp again. He had even organized the den on the first floor.

It wasn't natural for a bachelor to be so neat. I was beginning to hate this guy. I untucked the sheets on the beds, raised the toilet seats, and put smudges on the dining room table.

When I went down to the basement and saw what was down there, I hated him even more, but for very different reasons.

The stairway ran along one wall. No walls divided the basement, leaving an open space the same size as the upper floors. At the edge of the red beam of light, I saw four wooden eight-by-eights. These supported the upper floor. In the center of the basement stood a long, black, wooden table.

Walking over, I saw it had a lip around the edge and a drain (dumping into a bucket) on one end. Attached to each end were ropes.

I finally found where they murdered Lila.

I switched the red lens on the flash for the regular one. Under white light the table was not completely black. On the surface of the table, was a star with a circle around it and strange, wavy symbols around that.

Farther back, there were empty animal pens and cages along one wall. Along the wall opposite the stairs were shelves and a display of knives and other tools. Knives with wavy blades, curved blades and knives I didn't know existed. The tools weren't the sort of thing you'd find at a hardware store. They were the kind you'd find in the personal collection of Vlad the Impaler.

The shelves held jars containing a clear fluid and bits and pieces of animals. June Kayer got off easy. There were plenty of other animal parts here that could have ended up in her fridge.

But the prizes of Davison's collection were a pair of jars labeled: L. Glisan. One held a clear fluid and a tongue. The other was full of blood.

That's when I heard the front door slam.

CHAPTER 43

Cornered

I couldn't tell how many people were upstairs. It was at least two, could be three or more. Nor could I make out any of the voices or conversation, but it sounded like they were in the kitchen.

There wasn't anyplace to hide. In one corner was a furnace, but there was no room there. The animal pens would do nothing but corner me for them. Funny how a confined space will do that. The table wouldn't provide much protection. Unless I managed to disguise myself as a disemboweled body.

That left the windows.

They couldn't open enough for me to climb out. The well outside the window was too small to allow a quick escape, which I would need if I broke the window.

I guess I was going to have to hide out in the open. There were four lights hanging from the ceiling. I removed the bulbs from three of the lamps and slipped them in my suit pockets. Then I eased my .45 out of the holster and clicked it off safe.

I didn't have to wait long.

The door at the top of the stairs opened, sending light and shadows down the stairs. I moved away from the furnace to look around the stairs at the shadows before the door closed. I didn't have any better idea how many people there were.

When the door closed, a flickering yellow glow replaced the steady white light. I moved further back into the shadows.

"What are you guys doing to me? I did everything you wanted." I couldn't see anyone yet, but that sounded like the Chief.

"You called off the IA investigation of Hayden. We mean to show you that you do what we tell you or else." This was a muffled voice.

"He shot the hell out of a cop car! Besides, the frame-up never would have stood up in court. Let me go."

"We'll never know about the frame up will we?"

Four people were stepping off the stairs. Except Bowers, all wore robes and masks. The figures at the front and rear of the column carried a candle. Bowers was in the middle. He wore a blindfold and hand cuffs. One of the robed figures guided him down the stairs.

The two with the candles, lit two more candles fixed to the pillars. Then they put their candles in brackets on the other two pillars. The brackets had reflectors, directing the light to the table. I still had some shadows to hide in.

Bower's escort took off his blindfold. Looking at the table the chief asked, "What's going on here? What are you doing?"

"We are going to show you what happens when you don't obey the Cadre." It was his escort who had been speaking. One of the candle bearers joined chief Bowers and the speaker. The other candle bearer walked to the knives hanging on the wall.

"You can't do this to me. Let me go." The speaker drilled Bowers in the stomach. He doubled over. They put Bowers on the table. They put a strap across this chest. Next they tied his legs. Last the speaker took the bracelets off and they tied his wrists to the corners. The speaker took the cuffs off like an out of practice pro. This was Largo.

Bowers was catching his breath while they finished staking him out. The cat looking at the knives had made a choice and went back to the table. This had to be Davison.

He had chosen a large, sharp looking knife. He used the blade to reflect light into Bowers' eyes. Bowers thrashed on the table. "I'm sorry. It won't happen again. I'll do whatever you say."

Davison lowered the knife to Bowers' groin, leaving it there for a few seconds. He then moved the knife up like he was going to stick it in the chiefs gut. Instead, he sliced Bower's shirt The chief was a statue, trying to keep the knife from nicking him. I was right about the blade. It cut through the shirt like it was cutting through water.

With the shirt out of the way, Davison passed the knife over Bowers' chest. The chief let out a whimpering moan. Chicken.

He didn't have anything to worry about. There was no bucket beneath the drain to collect the blood. They were playing him like Galileo. Show him the tools of the trade and wait for him to crack.

"Well Largo, I thought Rose and Thistle was a gentleman's club. I didn't know you guys were into anything like this." All the faces turned in my direction, but none looked straight at me. They didn't know where I was.

"Hayden, is that you?" asked the speaker, his hands moved inside his robe. The figure by his side was doing the same. Was this Vincent? "Now you know everything. Let's talk this over."

I didn't respond. I was moving through the shadows. It must have worked, because they kept their eyes on the corner. Largo started moving to the shadows near the stairs. That was smart, cut off my escape. Too bad I was going the other way, toward the shelves.

"Hayden, you've got to help me. The frame-up wasn't my idea. I didn't want anything to do with it."

"Shut up you," said Davison. He put his knife to Bower's throat.

Vinny remained in the light. He finally cleared his gun from his robe. I couldn't see his dad through the shadows, pillars, and everything else. As if on cue they both started to throw metal into the furnace corner. When Vinny brought up his roscoe, I closed my eyes and turned my head away. I didn't want their muzzle flash to ruin my night vision.

The world became one of sound. Sound you could almost feel. The gunfire sounded like thunder in a box canyon. The sounds echoed several times off the concrete walls. The sheet metal of the furnace rang with each bullet that punched a hole in it.

When the cacophony ended, I looked back, bringing the automatic around. I found my target and squeezed off two rounds. Vinny dropped without a sound, not even a moan.

Largo returned fire, but his shots were wild. He didn't know where my shots came from and he had no night vision. Mine wasn't much better. I had two bright white afterimages floating in front of my face. I had closed one eye while shooting. I opened it now and closed the other. It wasn't great, but it helped.

I was feeling my way along the shelves as I heard shells clinking together. Largo was reloading. He might not have fired all his lead, but like a good Marine he was going into combat with a fully loaded weapon. I chose not to reload. Like a good soldier, what I aim at, I kill.

Small sounds escaped past Bowers' throat. He wanted to watch the action. He didn't want his throat sliced. Davison's eyes darted about trying to find me. He wasn't my concern. I didn't know where Largo was.

I took one bulb out of my pocket, tossing it to one side of the basement. Its pop was almost lost to my ringing ears. Largo fired at the sound.

The afterimage wasn't as bad this time. He was across from me, on the other side of the table, and the lit candles. I did this twice more, each bulb going to a different corner. Largo fired twice more. His flashes changed location as he pivoted around his center of mass.

Most guys brought souvenirs from the war. Some brought guns home. For others it was Nazi stuff. Then there were the few who brought back a superstition. They believed that lighting three cigarettes on one match was bad luck. In a way they were right.

German snipers watching American positions watched for the flame of a match. The first cigarette the GI lit caught the sniper's attention. The second, and the sniper took aim. The third, and there was a dead GI.

When Largo fired the third time, there was a dead scumbag.

The smell of cordite hung heavy in the air. My ears rang. My eyes saw exploding flashes of light, and my head pounded.

Davison stood in the ring of flickering light. I couldn't see his face because of the mask. He kept looking from my direction to the bodies still in the shadows.

I said, "I guess they didn't want to answer my question about Rose and Thistle being a gentleman's club. How does butchering people bring you power?"

"Power is only part of it. We are paving the way for our master. He requires sacrifices to show our dedication to him and his cause." Was it a rule that pathologists be nuts?

"What are you doing Hayden? Shoot him. That's an order!" said Bowers. I ignored him.

"That's the reason you chopped her up and tortured her?"

"That and to send a message to the others who wanted to leave or talk about us."

"Who ordered it? Largo?"

"Yes. He was the leader of our group. But there are more."

"There's more groups?"

"More than you know. Our work does not end here." He looked again at the bodies. "But I guess I'm out of options."

"You could put down the knife and then I'll get some guys with butterfly nets to take you to a nice, soft room."

"I'm not crazy!" His knife wavered over Bowers.

"That's obvious to me. Hell, I have a collection of fly's wings that I've kept since elementary. But there are people who would disagree.

"Don't talk to me like that. Doctor Burkholter doesn't care that you pick on him, but I do. So stop it."

"For Christ's sake! Shoot him!" piped up Bowers. It wasn't a good idea. Davison looked down at his captive. He grabbed the knife in both hands raising it over his head.

"Don't say that name." I plugged him before the good doctor could bring down the knife.

I hated to do it. I wanted to find out more about Rose and Thistle. I wanted to know who else was in the Cadre, as Largo called it. But I have a feeling that Davison didn't know anyone else. Largo was this group's connection to the others.

At least this way, I saved the taxpayers the cost of a trial.

"Nice work Hayden. I guess this clears most everything up." Captain Bartholomew stepped into the ring of light.

CHAPTER 44

The Negotiation

"You involved in this too, Cap?"

"No. I thought about our talk today. I wasn't any better than any of them if I knew who was behind this, but I wasn't willing to help." He walked farther into the circle. His hands hung at his side, in plain view. They were empty. "Bart. Glad you're here. Untie me. Hayden wants to hide in the dark over there." Cap looked down at him, a sad smile on his face.

"I followed Largo. His son and Dr. Davison already had the Chief. I waited outside until I heard the gunshots. I thought I heard sounds coming from the basement, but I couldn't tell what was going on, so I waited to see who came up. Then I heard your voice."

He looked at the bodies. "Which one was Largo?"

"Behind you," I said. He looked and bent over the body. I moved through the dark in case he was going to try something.

"I'm sorry it came to this old friend, but you had to know that I couldn't let you get away with it." He stood. His hands weren't empty, he held the mask.

His face still held that sad smile. "What's next?"

"You can let me go."

"This is Hayden's case. I assigned it to him. I can't take it away now." I stepped into the light, my gun at my side.

"He has to leave the force." I nodded to Bowers.

"Why?" I drew out the pictures, tossing them on the chief.

"He's compromised. We can't trust him."

"It's an indiscretion. Come on Hayden, I dropped the IA case. We're square now. What was I supposed to do? She threw herself at me."

"Did she hold a gun to your head? If she did, I'd like to know where she was hiding it."

"It was sex, it didn't mean anything."

"That's why you're tied up? Because it was sex, it didn't mean anything? They had a big hold on you for nothing."

"He's right chief, you've got to go."

"You can't do this to me."

"Bullshit. You did it to yourself. You showed that you have a price. How can anyone trust you again? You're off the force or the other photos end up in the wrong hands."

"Now you're blackmailing me."

"You did it to yourself." Bowers closed his eyes in thought.

"What about my pension."

"You don't mind if he retires do you Hayden?"

"I'd rather he go without, but I can keep from singing as long as he's gone." Bowers looked up at me pleading. "I'm holding the other photos. If you ever show up in public life again, they go public too."

Bowers deflated.

"Said your peace?" Cap asked.

"I've said enough."

"Why don't you go on? Chief Bowers and I have some business to discuss. Then we'll get this place taken care of."

When I reached the stairs, Cap asked, "Do you want a promotion?"

"If it happens, I want it to be because I earned it."

I went upstairs and cooled my heels.

CHAPTER 45

Bent Cops

I went out through the front doorway. The shattered door hung from the hinges. Cap must have busted it in at the same time someone fired. That or my ears had been ringing so bad that I didn't hear it.

On the front step, I took a deep breath of the clear night air. The grey clouds that had hung over the city all day had moved off to the east, leaving the night sky in full view.

It's not the way I wanted things to work out. I wanted a chance to find out who else was in Rose and Thistle. On the bright side, I did manage to clear up Lila's murder. I guess that would have to be enough. I sighed and moved off to my car.

Lost in my own thoughts, I hardly noticed the radio traffic. My hand was on the knob to turn it off, when I heard, "disturbance at Evergreen Terrace." That was Nora's neighborhood.

As I raced through the streets of town, the radio told me what was happening in short, ragged dispatches. There had been a shooting and an ambulance was on the way.

Davison's house was to the east of town. Nora lived to the west. I had a river to cross, traffic to avoid and adrenaline to control.

The details over the radio were sketchy. I only knew that there was a shooting and the ambulance was going back to the hospital empty. A hearse and the ME had been called. At the same time, Cap called in his scene. Two killings and only one ME left.

The bubble light on the dash painted everything in my way with red light. This and the wail of siren and screeching of tires told people to stay out of my way.

By the time I tore into Nora's neighborhood, I knew the shooting had been at her house. I didn't know who the hearse was for.

I parked as close as I could, got out and brushed past newshawks and curious citizens. A uniformed let me past the parameter. Sgt. Langella stopped me outside the house.

"We gotta stop meeting like this detective."

"What happened?"

"The private cop you hired shot it out with a couple of bulls, only they weren't here on official business."

"Is she . . . "

"Your dame and the shamus are fine. They're questioning them in the house now. I don't know what you told him, but the private won't leave her side until you get in there. They want to take him to Central for questioning but nothing short of a bullet or sap poison is going to make him leave."

"Was it Andrews and Willis?"

"How'd you know?"

"I get paid to make little birds sing." I thanked him and he stepped aside, allowing me in the house.

The living room was a confusion of cops, photographers and lab guys. Andrews and Willis still lay on the floor in a pool of their own blood. Someone pointed me to the kitchen. That's where they were questioning Nora and Spragg.

When I walked in the kitchen all eyes turned to me. Nora looked at me almost like she didn't quite believe I was alive, that I could be alive. She looked to Spragg as if searching for answers then jumped up and ran to my arms.

It took several hours to get everyone out of the house. The detectives didn't want to leave. It was hard for them to believe that it was a justified killing. Most cops don't believe that some cops are bad news. They believe the tin gives them all the reason they need to do anything they want. It finally took calling Davison's house and having them talk to Cap and the chief to get them to leave Spragg alone.

He was the last to leave. I walked him out the door. On the front porch I stuck out my hand and thanked him.

"For what? I did what you paid me to do." He switched the cigar stub from one side of his mouth to the other.

"You didn't have to stay until I got here."

He took the cigar out of his mouth and gestured with it. "If the play was the other way around, would you leave my dame alone?" I nodded then settled up the account.

"In a few days, you'll get a big manila envelope in the mail from me. Give me a call and I'll swing by to pick it up." He nodded, then walked off in the dark to his car.

Nora packed up what she needed and we went to a hotel. The guy at the counter didn't like us checking in so late at night. He looked at our fingers and didn't see any rings. Greenbacks won out in the end.

In the room, I finally got the whole story. Around nightfall Nora went out to Spragg's car asking him if he wanted to come in for dinner. She was afraid to be in the house alone, so she asked him to stay inside until I got back.

About the time I was shooting it out with Largo, she went to bed. Twenty minutes later, the sound of gunfire woke her up. Spragg was sitting on the front room sofa in the dark when Andrews and Willis jimmied the lock on the front door. Spragg challenged them and they opened fire and lost.

I have to guess that they were going to kill her to send me a message. They should have tried a phone call.

CHAPTER 46

The Debt

The rain of the previous day was gone and I soaked up some sun while waiting for someone to answer my knock on the door. The butler did it.

"Oh, detective. Senator Glisan is waiting for you." The house was as I remember: enough mahogany to choke a beaver and classical music in the background. It was Chopin this time.

"You tell him about Lila's house?"

"I did."

"And you still have your job. Do you think you would if I had to tell him."

"No. Senator Glisan values honesty and forthrightness."

"He in the office?"

"Yes." He took my hat.

"Thanks, I can find it myself. If I get lost, I'll follow my ear." I moved down the hall. He was waiting for me. He stood and shook my hand.

"I read the paper, nice work. I appreciate what you did." I had something to tell him. It must have showed. "What's wrong?"

I told him the story, from beginning to end. I told him the things the newspaper didn't cover. I told him the things that didn't make it into the reports.

And I told him the things I knew, but couldn't prove.

I don't do this for every case I work. And I didn't do this because of who he was. I did it because I owed it to him. If he hadn't used some of his muscle downtown, I could have been in jail or dead or both. I did it because I thought it would cover the debt.

When I finished, he studied the surface of his desk. He put a hand over his eyes. When his eyes returned to mine, they were stone and his jaw muscles bulged as if under some massive strain.

"This group, this Rose and Thistle, Largo was its leader?"

"If I were a betting man, I'd bet everything I own that he wasn't. I think he was the highest ranking member in the department, but I can't be sure."

"How do we find other members?"

"You could track down everyone who ever graduated from Downing and beat a confession out of them. From what I can tell, few graduates actually belong to the group or Cadre as Largo called it." Glisan chewed on that for a few moments.

"What about this George Fox? Am I or some other little girl's father going to have to worry about him?"

"He knows I'm keeping an eye on him. Besides, Rose and Thistle gave him a good scare. He's going to behave himself."

"It's tough to hear about Lila like this. I should have paid more attention. I thought Sally was a good friend, I had no idea she would get her involved with something like this."

What do you say to that? I could have placated him. I could have told him that kids do stupid things. Saying that would have been stupid. Besides, he didn't want an answer.

"In a few days, you'll get an envelope from me in the mail. If you'll give me a call at the office, I'll swing by and get it."

"Why did you send it to me?"

"You had the juice to do something about it within the system. Spragg had the juice do something outside the system."

"You should be a politician Hayden."

"I don't like babies enough to be near them, let alone kiss them." I stood.

"Thanks Hayden," Glisan said, standing. He held out a thick envelope.

"You know I can't take that."

"You stuck your neck out farther for my daughter than you needed to. I'm afraid many cops would have turned tail."

"I hope not." He still held the envelope out. "You want to give it to someone who could use it, send it to June Kayer at Downing. Her old man was a cop who would have done the same as I did."

He smiled. "I figured it would work out that way." We said our good byes and I went to get my hat.

CHAPTER 47

Epilogue

I couldn't remember the last time I'd worn my blues. I hated it. It was a warm spring day, nearing the eighties. I was thinking of the rain a few days ago during Lila's funeral.

The uniform of the day was the wool long sleeved shirt, wool pants, the stupid service cap and white gloves.

Here I was, being a pallbearer for Largo. It was a cruel joke. Bowers had insisted that I do this.

As far as the public knew, Davison was the only one responsible for Lila's murder. Largo had helped me track down Davison. In an ugly gun battle, we killed the doctor, unfortunately, both Largo and his son also died in the shoot out.

At least the chief would be gone at the end of the week.

Cap and Bowers must have had a long talk that night. After the funeral Bowers was going to announce that Cap was going to be the new Chief of Detectives. The city gave me a commendation for solving the case and for "bravery above and beyond the call of duty."

Also, Bowers had found it in his heart not to press charges against Sally Kaufman. Since I didn't need her as a witness anymore and I couldn't connect her to any other crimes, she was free to go from the poor farm. I drove out to pick her up after leaving her out there for several days.

The experience must have done her some good. She didn't want to leave. She has started volunteering out there. She promised me that she was through with Rose and Thistle.

Nancy Mason was also done with the Cadre. To make sure she doesn't have any problems, she's moving out of state. She told me where, but that's a secret I'm going to keep.

Nora's grandmother is back in town. I'm supposed to go out to dinner with them. They are staying at a hotel downtown provided by the department. It was the least they could do after two of their officers tried to kill Nora. Once the department finishes the repairs, Granny is going to sell the place.

Representatives from police and sheriff departments from several states attended. There were also many civic leaders. I also saw a few Marine uniforms.

At the end of the funeral an older man walked over and stuck out his hand.

"Detective Hayden, congratulations. " I took his hand. My picture had been in the paper a lot recently, I figured that's how he knew me.

I mumbled thanks and tried to let go. His hand gripped tighter and he bent his head close to mine.

"Facta non verba."

"What? How do you know that?" The department kept that out of the paper.

"No, the proper response is, 'Ad nocendum potentes.' Have a good life Hayden. We're watching you."

He slipped his hand away from mine and disappeared into the crowd.

Dennis Mossburg is an up-and-coming author with a passion for noir and suspense. His debut novel, "The Demise of the Dame," is an exciting mystery that explores the darker side of celebrity. With his background in criminal justice, Dennis keeps readers on the edge of their seats.

Dennis' previous work is, *Reflections on Leadership, What Leaders say about Leadership*. Dennis is working on his next project which explores the thin line between life and death. He lives in Eastern Washington with his wife and their dogs.

Follow him on Facebook. His email is Dennis.Mossburg@gmail.com.